A thrilling new trilogy from Harlequin Presents and Harlequin Medical Romance!

Royally Tempted

...at the first incendiary glance!

Castilona royals are used to unimaginable wealth and privilege, so when one falls ill, only the best treatment the island kingdom's coffers can buy will do. But a visit to Clínica San Carlos may change the course of the monarchy's future...

When King Octavio spent one red-hot night in the comforting arms of hospital cleaner Phoebe, he never anticipated her falling pregnant—with twins. The only reasonable royal solution? Demanding her hand in marriage!

Twins for His Majesty by Clare Connelly

Available now from Harlequin Presents!

Princess Xiomara will only allow the world's top fetal surgeon to treat her cousin's wife and the kingdom's unborn heirs. Even if Dr. Edmund ignites her deepest desires...

Forbidden Fling with the Princess by Amy Andrews

When a hurricane hits, head of hospital security— Xiomara's illegitimate half brother—Xavier and clinical director Lola are stuck at Clínica San Carlos overnight. With a storm of passion raging between them!

One Night to Royal Baby by JC Harroway

Both available now from Harlequin Medical Romance!

Dear Reader,

Writing can be solitary work, so when two other Harlequin author friends, Clare Connelly and Amy Andrews, asked me to collaborate on linked stories set in the same world, I jumped at the chance. We created the stunning Mediterranean island kingdom of *Castilona* and wove our individual stories together to create characters that span all three books. With *One Night to Royal Baby*, I was tasked to wrap up the trilogy with Lola and Xavier's love story. I hope you enjoy escaping to the Mediterranean with them as they weather cyclone Gabriel and their rocky road to love and happily-ever-after.

Love, *JC* x

ONE NIGHT TO ROYAL BABY

JC HARROWAY

MEDICAL ROMANCE

If you purchased this book without a cover you should be aware that this book is stolen property. It was reported as "unsold and destroyed" to the publisher, and neither the author nor the publisher has received any payment for this "stripped book."

Harlequin® MEDICAL ROMANCE

ISBN-13: 978-1-335-99324-3

One Night to Royal Baby

Copyright © 2025 by JC Harroway

All rights reserved. No part of this book may be used or reproduced in any manner whatsoever without written permission.

Without limiting the author's and publisher's exclusive rights, any unauthorized use of this publication to train generative artificial intelligence (AI) technologies is expressly prohibited.

This is a work of fiction. Names, characters, places and incidents are either the product of the author's imagination or are used fictitiously. Any resemblance to actual persons, living or dead, businesses, companies, events or locales is entirely coincidental.

For questions and comments about the quality of this book, please contact us at CustomerService@Harlequin.com.

TM and ® are trademarks of Harlequin Enterprises ULC.

Harlequin Enterprises ULC
22 Adelaide St. West, 41st Floor
Toronto, Ontario M5H 4E3, Canada
www.Harlequin.com

HarperCollins Publishers
Macken House, 39/40 Mayor Street Upper
Dublin 1, D01 C9W8, Ireland
www.HarperCollins.com

Printed in U.S.A.

Lifelong romance addict **JC Harroway** took a break from her career as a junior doctor to raise a family and found her calling as a Harlequin author instead. She now lives in New Zealand and finds that writing feeds her very real obsession with happy endings and the endorphin rush they create. You can follow her at jcharroway.com and on Facebook, X and Instagram.

Books by JC Harroway

Harlequin Medical Romance

A Sydney Central Reunion

Phoebe's Baby Bombshell

Buenos Aires Docs

Secretly Dating the Baby Doc

Gulf Harbour ER

Tempted by the Rebel Surgeon
Breaking the Single Mom's Rules

Jet Set Docs

One Night to Sydney Wedding

Sexy Surgeons in the City

Manhattan Marriage Reunion

Nurse's Secret Royal Fling
Forbidden Fiji Nights with Her Rival
The Midwife's Secret Fling

Visit the Author Profile page
at Harlequin.com for more titles.

To AA and CC, if only the gorgeous Mediterranean
kingdom we created existed off the page...
Perfect location for a field trip!

**Praise for
JC Harroway**

"JC Harroway has firmly cemented her place as one of
my favourite Harlequin Medical Romance authors with
her second book in the imprint and with wonderful
characters and a heart-melting and very sexy romance
set in the beautiful Cotswolds."
—*Goodreads* on *How to Resist the Single Dad*

CHAPTER ONE

Dr Lola Garcia read her typed letter of resignation, her mouse hovering over the send button. As clinical director of *Clinico San Carlos*, an exclusive private hospital renowned for world class care, she answered only to the board of directors, astute businesspeople who would likely thank her for her years of service while swiftly and efficiently appointing her successor. But even as restlessness tugged increasingly at her consciousness, she glanced around her well-appointed office, thinking of her achievements in building the clinic's current reputation.

Just because she secretly hankered for a new challenge, maybe to make a difference in the less privileged parts of society, didn't mean her position there wouldn't be highly coveted. The island kingdom of Castilona was the Mediterranean's jewel in the crown. Her job would be snapped up in a heartbeat.

A knock sounded at her office door. Lola

quickly locked her computer screen, the message unsent, and sat a little straighter.

'Come in,' she called, glancing up expectantly.

The door swung open and Xavier Torres, head of hospital security, filled the doorway. His dark brooding stare, broad shoulders and imposing height were enough to make even the toughest of villains hesitate. He wore slim-fit black trousers and a matching polo shirt bearing the hospital's logo, which hugged his athletic build in a way that made Lola aware of how long it had been since she'd last gone on a date. But regardless of her attraction to the man their interactions during the six months they'd worked together had remained polite, professional and never too friendly.

'Xavier, come in.' Discretely clearing her throat, which always seemed to clamp up when speaking to this strong silent hulk of a man, Lola stood and offered him a seat.

'Thank you, Dr Garcia.' He eyed the chair but declined with a tilt of his strong, clean-shaven jaw.

'I've told you before...' she smiled patiently, her body tingling with the awareness of him, '...you're welcome to call me Lola away from our clients.' The 'clients' being the hospital's private and wealthy patients.

She'd yet to persuade him to drop the formality. When they first met Xavier had worked as part of the royal family's personal protection detail, accompanying Princess Xiomara and Dr Edmund

Butler, the world-renowned expert on intrauterine endoscopic laser surgery, to the clinic.

Lola's instantaneous attraction to Xavier had been easily dismissed. Her high professional standards were legendary and were directed nowhere more vigorously than towards herself. Her career was everything. She'd once even chosen it over marriage to a man she'd believed she'd loved.

'Yes, Dr Garcia,' he said, staring at the window behind her head while standing with his hands behind his back in that habitual way of his that reminded her that he'd once been in the Castilonian army before he was discharged on medical grounds.

Perhaps he hoped the stance would help him blend into the background. A skill handy while working for the royal family. But Xavier Torres' presence was far too electrifying for him to be invisible. He filled up any room he was in with his magnetic aura.

'I wondered if we might discus the weather, ma'am,' he went on.

'The weather?' Lola concealed a sigh. The only thing that grated more than his refusal to use her first name was when he called her *ma'am*. It made her feel…ancient. And asexual! And with him around, she felt every inch a woman in her sexual prime. Maybe that was the reason for her restlessness—her self-imposed lack of a personal life.

She glanced at the window where a constant

deluge of rain had turned the normally crystal-blue sea and sky to grey.

'Yes. Cyclone Gabriel,' he said.

Rather than sit back down behind her desk, Lola perched on the front edge facing him. 'I thought the forecast predicted it would blow east.'

Tropical-like cyclones or *medicanes*—a portmanteau of Mediterranean and hurricane—usually occurred at this time of year, although rarely.

'The latest indications are that wind directions have changed and it's heading straight for us,' he said, finally meeting her stare, his unreadable as usual. 'I suggest we prepare for worst case scenarios, ma'am. In my experience it's better to be safe than sorry.'

Lola shuddered at the moment's exhilaration that occurred when their eyes met. But there were always more important matters to address than her love life, or sad lack of one, an impending cyclone an excellent case in point.

'Yes, I agree,' Lola said, her mind racing through lists of possible contingencies. 'Let's make sure we're prepared.' She stood, setting aside her irrelevant attraction to the clinic's head of security. 'Please speak to maintenance and ensure the hospital's backup generators are ready to go in case of a power cut.'

'Yes, ma'am.' He jerked his chin in a nod.

She rounded her desk and reached for her

mouse to wake up her computer. 'I'll speak to each head of department and suggest that all superfluous staff be sent home to be with their families before the storm strikes. We can manage for one night with a skeleton staff.'

'Yes, ma'am.' Rather than leave her office, he hesitated, his lips pressed together, a minute clenching of the muscles of his jaw. Then he met her stare once more, and she saw the concern he usually did well to hide whenever some metaphorical fire or other required extinguishing. Like her, he took his work very seriously.

'Was there something else?' she asked, grateful he was so good at his job. Excellent in fact. She suspected this role at the clinic wouldn't satisfy him for long or challenge him sufficiently. There was a restless, prowling quality to him that made her curious to know about his private life, his past and his dreams. Not that there'd ever been the time or opportunity for that. It was just as well. She'd devoted herself to her career these past fourteen years since breaking off her engagement to Nicolás.

'No, ma'am.'

'Don't worry, Xavier,' she said. 'We are built to last. This building was once a medieval monastery. It's been here for centuries, I'm sure it can weather the storm. And at least we haven't the acute and emergency admissions of the public hospital to worry about.'

Xavier nodded once more and turned for the door.

'Wait,' she said, stalling him. 'Can you please make a call to your counterpart at St Sebastian's?' she asked, referring to the larger fully public hospital. 'And I'll do the same. Offer them any support or extra equipment they might need and liaise with our porters to transport items there before the weather deteriorates further and the storm arrives in earnest.'

'Yes, Dr Garcia.'

'And Xavier, if you need to be elsewhere, you can head home too. We should be fine with only one security guard tonight.'

'I'd prefer to stay,' he said. 'To ensure everyone remains safe.'

'Very well.' Lola nodded, wondering again at his relationship status. Did he—like her with the exception of her cat Albie— live alone?

'Should *you* leave in case the coastal roads become inundated?' he said, a flattering hint of concern in his eyes.

'I prefer to stay too,' she said, her stomach fluttering. She was fiercely independent, once rejecting a married life of wealth and status to pursue her career because her fiancé had, rather chauvinistically, insisted she couldn't do both. She'd never regretted that choice. But for some reason seeing that this man cared for her welfare brought a return of the discontent that had prompted her letter of resignation.

'I'm the clinical director,' she said finally. 'The buck stops with me.'

Something like admiration flitted over his expression. 'Then let's prepare for whatever the night might hurl at us,' he said confidently, as if he could handle anything.

As the door snicked gently closed behind him, Lola released another sigh, her thoughts returning to the wellbeing and safety of everyone under her care—staff and patients alike. Yes, hopefully, no matter what Cyclone Gabriel threw at them, *Clinico San Carlos* would remain as steady and immovable as their mysterious head of security.

CHAPTER TWO

THREE HOURS LATER, as night fell, Xavier's gut feeling about the storm had proved accurate. While for now, all seemed calm and business as usual inside the hospital's sturdy stone walls, outside Cyclone Gabriel rattled the entire island as if Castilona, from its coastal fishing towns to its mountainous and forested interior, were trapped inside a vigorously shaken snow globe.

From the security office adjacent to the hospital's reception, where his colleague Antonio was stationed, Xavier listened to the live news feed and weather reports, unease building as he anticipated a night of damage limitation. The rain, present for most of the day, had turned torrential. Reports of flash flooding and land slips all over the island made news. Tidal surges had taken out the main coastal road between the clinic and the island's main port, *Puerto Reyes.* Several fishing boats had been torn from their moorings and smashed onto the rocks. Wind gusts of up to a hundred miles per hour were ripping terracotta tiles from rooftops, felling trees as if they were matchsticks and causing all sorts of infrastructure issues.

Having heard enough bad news, Xavier left the office to perform his rounds. He was about to head to the lower ground floor to check on the kitchen staff who'd stayed behind to cater for the patients and staff working the night shift, when the emergency pager he wore on his belt at all times, whether he was on duty or not because he liked to be kept aware of everything that happened at the clinic, screeched out an alarm. A cardiac arrest call on the post-op ward.

Xavier took off running, his military training kicking in. He arrived at the emergency breathless from taking the stairs at full pelt, but mentally calm and able to quickly assess the situation.

Directed by one of the nurses, he entered the private room occupied by a retired statesman from a neighbouring European country who'd recently undergone a plastic surgery procedure at the clinic. Lola was already there. Dressed in the same elegant trouser suit she'd worn all day, she was kneeling on the edge of the bed performing chest compressions on the unconscious patient.

Sensing him enter she glanced over her shoulder, her stare revealing she was relieved to see him.

'Is there anything I can do to help?' he asked, noting that wisps of her normally immaculate chestnut brown hair had escaped her tight bun and her cheeks were flushed from exertion.

'Can you take over here?' she asked without a second's hesitation, her voice calm and in charge.

Xavier nodded, glad that he could be of some use. But of course, she knew his history. Knew he had medical training from his time in the army. And everyone employed at *Clinico San Carlos* had undergone mandatory CPR training prior to commencing work.

Xavier relieved her of her efforts with the chest compressions, quickly scanning the room to find that while there were two ward nurses present, Lola was the only doctor.

Lola stepped aside and Xavier timed his chest compressions to coincide with the nurse inflating the man's lungs with a bag resuscitator.

'He's in asystole,' Lola said, meeting Xavier's stare, letting him know that the heart showed no sign of electrical activity and was in an unshockable rhythm that didn't require defibrillation.

'Does he have a cardiac history?' Lola asked the nurse as she prepared a syringe of adrenaline.

'No. His only medical history is diabetes,' the nurse confirmed.

Lola checked her watch. 'Check for a pulse please,' she instructed, supervising the arrest protocol now that she was free from administering the chest compressions.

Xavier felt the man's neck for a carotid pulse

and Lola did the same on the other side, their eyes meeting after a second. Xavier shook his head, his respect for this woman multiplying. Over the past six months, he'd come to see that she ran the *Clinico San Carlos* with the utmost professionalism and integrity. No detail was too minor to escape her notice. Every staff member, from the cleaners to the consultants, was treated equally. Under Lola Garcia's clinical directorship, patient care featured at the forefront of her every decision.

To say he found her fascinating, and a little intimidating, would be an understatement.

'Resume CPR,' she said, administering adrenaline into the man's IV cannula, her expression carefully devoid of emotion.

But inside, she must be concerned for this elderly man. Not that she wasn't fully capable of dealing with any medical emergency. But maybe because Xavier was a soldier, maybe because he'd seen the worst and the best of humanity through his work, he recognised the hint of fear and concern in Lola's amber eyes. Like most, Lola Garcia had probably gone into medicine to help people. Losing a patient, tonight of all nights when they were operating under special circumstances, would take its toll. No matter how calm and efficient she appeared under pressure.

After another three minutes of resuscitation where the man's heart remained stubbornly unresponsive, they repeated the cycle. Pausing to check for a spontaneous pulse and respiration. Administering more adrenaline to try and restart the heart. And resuming CPR. With every cycle, Lola looked to him, her expression growing more desolate. Xavier tried to convey his non-verbal support, but after another ten minutes of futile efforts, the atmosphere in the room turned heavy and sombre, all eyes looking to Lola for guidance.

Xavier watched in growing empathy as Lola's shoulders slumped despondently. He shared her helplessness, but the situation was a sad fact of life. This patient had age and a pre-existing medical condition against him in addition to a recent general anaesthetic, which wasn't without risk. Of course, as the only doctor in the room, Lola would take full responsibility.

'Check for a pulse please,' Lola said, her voice thick with contained emotion. He and the nurse did as she asked, one by one shaking their heads to indicate that their efforts to revive the man had been in vain.

'I'm going to call it,' Lola said, bravely tilting up her chin. 'Any objections?' She glanced around the gathered staff who shook their heads.

No one ever wanted to give up CPR. But sometimes, despite everyone's best efforts, nothing more could be done to revive the patient. He'd essentially died the minute his heart and breathing had stopped.

Lola glanced at her watch. 'Please record time of death as twenty-one-forty-three.'

She swallowed and Xavier itched to put his hand out and touch her. To tell her she'd done a great job. But she wouldn't need his comfort. She was an intelligent and experienced physician. They weren't even friends. He'd deliberately kept his distance from day one on the job, knowing that his attraction to her was far too fierce and therefore dangerous. He only ever dated casually and Lola Garcia was a woman who epitomised every man's gold standard.

'I will personally inform Mr Ortega's next of kin,' she added, addressing the nurse who'd provided the patient's medical history.

As the team disbanded, returning to their other chores, Xavier hesitated. He watched a distracted Lola walk away from the ward, her posture ever so slightly less confident than usual.

Before he'd realised he'd moved, he sprinted after her. 'Dr Garcia…'

She turned, her dulled eyes lighting up expectantly. He hesitated, uncertain because as a result of his upbringing, he habitually kept people out emotionally. Having never known his father Xavier had grown up feeling as if he didn't fit. Anywhere. But his time in the army and his security work had taught him to put other people's safety and wellbeing above his own and he liked and respected Lola.

'You did everything you could,' he said, fighting the urge to touch her, as he'd been fighting it every day for months. Some attraction was just too powerful to be casual.

'I know.' She nodded, her stare dropping to the ground before meeting his. 'I'm not used to running the arrest protocol alone. But thanks for your help. I really appreciated it.'

Xavier said nothing. He might be calm in a crisis, but working so closely with a woman he felt thoroughly drawn to was bound to push him out of his comfort zone. Normally he avoided Lola Garcia like the plague. Not because she was an aloof or tyrannical boss. Quite the opposite in fact. The woman seemed to have a warm, open smile for everyone, while also managing to run the clinic with proficiency and professionalism. But there was something about her, beyond the fact that he found her incredibly attractive. He admired her. She was smart and intuitive and could relate to anyone with ease. Whereas Xavier considered himself an emotional island. As self-contained as Castilona itself. The island upon which he stood. The island he called home and had once patriotically considered it an honour to serve.

'I'd better call his family,' she said, her big brown eyes haunted as she turned away.

He watched her leave, torn. There was no place for dangerous personal interactions where Lola was concerned. She wasn't his usual type of woman. Even now, when his overriding instinct was to ensure she was okay after losing a patient, he knew he should leave well alone and walk away.

He had years of discipline training to fall back on, so ignoring her while the storm held them captive there should be a piece of cake. But he had a bad feeling about tonight and his gut was never wrong.

Back in her office, Lola hung up the phone, sighed and dropped her face into her hands, suddenly exhausted. She'd never grown used to breaking devastating news to a family member. In this instance, the patient's death was unexpected and therefore even more shocking.

Thinking back to the arrest, she recalled the same look of devastation on the faces of her team. Even stoical, unshakeable Xavier had been affected. That he'd reassured her afterwards had affected her just as deeply. Being trapped there overnight, the storm forcing them into a closer working relationship, she could no longer tolerate the polite but distant rapport they'd established over the past six months.

She needed to know this capable man better. Thinking about his calm, quiet strength, she removed the hair grips from her bun and brushed out her hair at the mirror in her en-suite bathroom. It had been a long time since any man had looked at her the way Xavier had as he'd checked up on her. Maybe even close to two years when she'd last dated. Did he find her attractive? Glancing at her slightly dishevelled appearance in the mirror, she wondered what he saw. At thirty-three, she kept fit and active. Her face was ordinary but symmetrical. Her dark hair thick and lustrous, considering she kept it tamed and professional Monday through Friday.

Just then, a knock at the door startled her. She automatically reached for the suit jacket she'd removed after returning to her office. Then she abandoned it once more reasoning the caller was unlikely to be a relative at this time of night, with the enforced hospital lockdown and the walls all but rattling under the force of the storm outside.

She opened the door to find Xavier once more on the threshold, her pulse accelerating excitedly. He wore a sheepish expression she'd never seen before and held out a small tray she recognised as coming from the kitchen, bearing a teapot, a cup and saucer and a milk jug.

'Is everything okay?' she asked, anticipating some other crisis because the cardiac arrest and phone call to Mr Ortega's brother had left her a little shaken.

'I... I brought you some tea,' he said with a frown that left her wondering if he regretted the thoughtful impulse.

'Thank you.' Touched, Lola self-consciously

ran a hand over her hair, which she usually always wore up for work. Maybe she should have slipped her heels back on before answering the door. Without them he seemed to tower over her. She stepped aside, forcing him to enter and place the tray where she indicated, on the coffee table in her office's seating area.

'You are a lifesaver, Xavier,' she said while he hesitated, clearly uncomfortable despite his thoughtful gesture.

'You look…tired,' he said his dark stare taking in her casual appearance. 'Is there somewhere you can get some rest?'

She looked down to see that her blouse had popped an extra button at the neckline, presumably when she'd been trying to restart Mr Ortega's heart.

'I'm okay.' She self-consciously refastened the tiny pearl button aware of the spicy scent of his aftershave. 'I'm just normally tucked up in bed by now with a cat curled up on my lap. Please join me,' she said refusing to take no for an answer. She collected a second cup and saucer from the sideboard before sinking into the sofa. 'I have a bad feeling that it's going to be a long night.'

She poured strong tea into the two cups while Xavier folded his big body into the armchair and accepted the cup and saucer, which looked ridiculously delicate in his large, manly hand.

'I share your intuition,' he said, sitting on the

edge of the chair as if ready to spring into action or escape.

'We've avoided getting friendly, you and I,' she said. 'I don't know anything personal about you. If we're going to spend the night here together, I'd like to know you a little better.'

Xavier froze, his expression comically horrified, as if he hated talking about himself.

'Are your loved ones safe tonight?' she asked, easing him into the conversation, eager to know him beyond what she could learn from his employment file.

He didn't wear a wedding ring and she'd never seen him so much as smile at any of the pretty young hospital staff, which only added to his mystique. Maybe he was like her, practically a workaholic.

'My mother is safe and sound at her home.' He held her stare, his expression settling to the bland neutral one he wore so often it could be a mask he slipped on with his uniform. 'She still lives on the palace estate, despite being retired, so she has someone she can call if she's concerned.'

'That's good.' Lola curled her feet up next to her. 'My parents and twin sister are in Spain, which is where I'm from, so I don't need to worry about them. And I live alone here. I'm hoping Albie, my cat, will have the good sense to wait out the storm curled up asleep.'

She paused, eyeing him over the rim of her cup

as she took another sip of tea. Her breathing a little faster as she waited for another exhilarating personal detail. She had of course memorised his employment record. He was Castilonian born and bred and had served ten years in the army before being medically discharged following a head injury that left him partially blinded. Upon which time he joined the royal family's personal protection detail protecting the King's cousin, Princess Xiomara.

'I also live alone,' he confirmed, his tea untouched. 'Not even a cat for company.'

'I hope you're not a workaholic like me?' Lola smiled, glad they had more in common than a professional desire to help others. 'Have you ever been married?'

She could no longer deny her curiosity for this wary and watchful man who clearly had many hidden talents beyond security.

'No. Have you?'

She shook her head. Her heart hammered that her curiosity was reciprocated. 'I was engaged once,' she admitted, 'but I called it off.' She placed her cup and saucer down on the coffee table. 'I was far too young, only nineteen. Nicolás came from a wealthy family and expected a traditional wife.' She made dismissive finger quotes around the last two words. 'Even back then I had ambitions beyond being a trophy or a puppet, hosting luncheons for the right people and running the domestic side of his ancient historic estate.'

His eyes narrowed, glittering with something like admiration. 'I'd say you made the right call.'

His comment, the implied compliment that she was good at her job, caught her off guard. 'Thank you. I really appreciated your calm competence earlier. Dr Lomas left to help out at St Sebastian's,' she said of their lead physician who would normally have answered the arrest call. 'I understand they've been inundated over there with storm-related admissions placing strain on the system.'

'I'm happy to help.' He took a swallow of tea and placed the cup on the coffee table. 'Although you didn't need me. You had the situation well in hand.'

Lola glanced at her lap to stop her from admitting how grateful she'd been when he'd shown up. There was something very lonely and desolate about emergencies that occurred in the middle of the night. An extra layer of responsibility. An awareness that there was no one else to call.

'Losing a patient never gets any easier,' she said, unexpectedly responding to his quiet strength, despite her usual self-sufficiency. 'The man most likely had a massive coronary event, or maybe a post-operative pulmonary embolism, but it's harder to accept when a death is…unexpected.'

'It was just timing.' His stare met hers, his dark

eyes penetrating, as if he saw her all too well. 'I doubt the outcome would have been different with a full complement of staff on board.'

She shrugged, saddened that in this instance, her best efforts to revive the patient hadn't been good enough.

'You disagree?' he challenged.

'No. I simply hate failure,' she admitted with a sigh. 'I'm a dreadful high-achiever, I'm afraid.' The standards she imposed, not only on her work at the clinic but also on herself, were perhaps a response to need to prove that her choice in giving up the life Nicolás had offered to pursue her career had been the right one.

'So, you were an army medic for a time?' she asked, changing the subject.

His company was easy and undemanding. There was something comforting and fascinating about him, as if he was exactly the right person to have around in a crisis. The storm, being trapped at work overnight, was making her unexpectedly uneasy.

'I was,' he replied, succinctly.

'Do you miss the…adrenaline?' she asked, secretly frustrated by his brief answer.

He tilted his head in challenge. 'My work here stimulates me sufficiently for now, otherwise I'd do something else.'

'Like what?' she asked, curious that she might have touched a nerve but finding his fortitude wildly attractive. Xavier Torres was not a man to be underestimated. He was clearly a man of action. A man comfortable in his own skin. 'You like to help people. To keep them safe.'

'Don't you?' he asked, his stare narrowing as if he found her equally fascinating.

She shifted, his observation making her flush. Were they finally going to acknowledge that their chemistry was mutual?

'I do,' she said. 'It's why I became a doctor. Although I never imagined I'd stay so long in *this* particular job.'

Surprise registered in his expression. 'Because it's lost its challenge?'

Lola's face heated that he'd been so perceptive. 'Don't get me wrong,' she said, 'I'm proud of what I've achieved here.'

'As you should be. You've made *Clinico San Carlos* a world class facility and attracted influential benefactors with bottomless pockets. Anyone who works in the health sector would agree that's no mean feat.'

'Thank you.' She accepted his compliment graciously.

'What else would you do?' he asked, his stare intense as if he couldn't bring himself to look away.

Wasn't that the million-dollar question? She shrugged, embarrassed that she had no definitive reply. 'Sometimes I have a hankering to help the other parts of society. Those…less affluent,' she said carefully. 'I'm proud of the public wards we have here. The free care we offer alongside the private. But I don't know… Lately I see myself doing something bold. Maybe working overseas for a medical relief charity.'

A few beats of silence followed her statement. His curious gaze sent more blood to her cheeks. She'd surprised him, that much she could tell. But otherwise, he was his usual hard to read self. His thoughts locked behind that dark, brooding stare of his.

Then he said, 'There are many ways to help others. You could do anything you chose, I'm sure.'

'So could you,' she countered, a delicious moment of understanding connecting them like a thread.

Suddenly, her skin became sensitive to every air current in the room, goosebumps raising on her arms as if they'd just admitted they wanted each other sexually.

Before either of them could say more or look away, a commotion sounded in the main foyer. Startled from what might have been an unsettling staring match, Lola rushed from her office with Xavier at her side.

The main entrance to the hospital was located across the marble-floored foyer. Still in her bare feet, Lola hurried towards the noise of someone pounding on the glass.

'Let me deal with this,' Xavier said, his hand on her arm drawing her to a halt before the hospital's security doors, where a soaking wet and bedraggled man was hammering at the glass with his balled fist.

'Someone must need help,' she said, hurrying after Xavier as he strode to the panel beside the door and inserted his master key to disarm the lock. 'He looks desperate.'

The minute the doors slid open to admit a blast of frigid air and driving rain, the man held out his arms, pleading. 'Please help me. It's my wife. She's injured.'

The frantic man indicated the car behind him, which was parked haphazardly, slanted across the circular cobbled driveway outside the clinic.

'We have a farm,' he explained. 'She was securing the animals. I came home from work to find her on the ground next to one of the sheds, which had been damaged by a fallen tree.'

In the passenger seat, sheltering from the torrential rain, sat a woman clutching a blood-stained towel to her forehead indicating an obvious head injury. And more alarming still, she was heavily pregnant.

Lola's heart leapt but she didn't hesitate. 'She's bleeding,' she told Xavier, urging him to assist the man. 'Help him bring her inside. They shouldn't try to make it to St Sebastian's in this weather. Not in her condition.'

Xavier rushed to the passenger side of car, while Lola retrieved a wheelchair from the porter's office behind reception. When all three of them had the woman transferred to the wheelchair and inside the warmth and shelter of the hospital, Xavier re-locked the doors and radioed for someone from maintenance to come and mop up the puddle of rain from the tiles.

'What's your name?' Lola asked the woman, quickly assessing her cognition and level of consciousness, her concerns that she'd sustained a significant head injury.

'Maria,' she said, clutching a towel stained with blood to her forehead. 'My husband's name is Diego.'

'Do you know where you are, Maria?' Lola asked, quickly taking her pulse.

'*Clinico San Carlos*,' the woman said, telling Lola she was aware of her surroundings.

Lola nodded and, after asking for permission, laid a hand over her abdomen to assess the tone of the uterus. It had been a while since she'd delivered a baby, but she could do it if she had to. 'Any pain or contractions? How many weeks are you?'

'No. I'm thirty-seven weeks,' Maria said.

'Did you black out?'

'I don't think so,' Maria said. 'I just saw stars

and it took me a while to get up, then I slipped back down in the mud and kind of gave up.'

'Okay, I need to take a closer look at your head. We'll take her to a treatment room,' she told Xavier. 'Would you mind collecting my theatre shoes from the closet in my office?' She was still barefooted.

While Maria's husband pushed the wheelchair, Lola directed them to a nearby fully equipped consultation room. Xavier quickly returned with her shoes and she slipped them on, feeling instantly more capable.

'Right, let's get you up on the bed,' she told Maria, pulling on some gloves.

Removing the sodden towel from Maria's hand, Lola revealed a six-centimetre gash at the woman's hair line. Without the pressure, the wound began to bleed heavily.

'This is going to require stitches I'm afraid,' Lola told Maria, glancing at Xavier. 'Can you unlock the drugs cupboard? I'll need local anaesthetic and antibiotics.'

Maybe it had been a mistake to let most of the staff go home. But during a state of emergency most people's thoughts turned to their family. If Lola had a husband and children she'd want to be home with them on a night like tonight making sure they were all safe.

'He's going,' Maria exclaimed, pointing to Diego. 'He's not good with blood.'

The husband wobbled unsteadily on his feet, bracing one arm on the wall. But before he could hit the floor in a faint, Xavier hauled him under the arms as if he weighed nothing.

'Let's sit you outside,' Xavier said. 'There's a couch. You can lie down until you feel better.'

Lola shot him a grateful glance. The last thing she needed were two head injuries to deal with.

When Xavier returned a few minutes later saying Diego was feeling better and sipping a glass of water, Lola put him to work. 'I'll need you to assist I'm afraid.'

'No problem.' He unlocked the drugs cupboard for her and washed his hands, pulling on his own pair of gloves.

'Can you keep the pressure on the wound?' she asked, passing him some sterile gauze.

Xavier did as she asked while Lola drew up the local anaesthetic in a syringe and poured iodine into a kidney dish.

'This might sting a little,' she said to Maria.

While Lola cleaned the wound, Xavier offered Maria his other hand. The woman took it gratefully and talked about her husband who'd been having Eye Movement Desensitization and Reprocessing or EMDR in order to overcome his fear of blood so he could attend the birth of their first child.

'He's going to be fine,' Xavier reassured her with a smile, taking her mind off the injection of local anaesthetic Lola placed around the wound. 'His most important role will be to hold your hand like I'm doing.'

He was such a natural leader. So good with people. Lola wanted to marvel at the rare sight of his smile but maintained her focus.

'Can you keep the pressure on either side of the wound while I suture?' Lola asked him, impressed when he did her bidding while still holding the patient's hand. Multitasking like a seasoned pro.

Together, they closed the wound and kept the patient's mind occupied with a steady flow of chatter. Then, while Lola completed a thorough examination of Maria's neurological system to exclude a significant head injury and took her blood pressure and temperature, Xavier went to the kitchen to make more tea. Lola watched him leave with a sigh. The man was a jack of all trades. Lola was so grateful for his calm reassuring presence. She had no idea what she'd have done without him tonight.

'I'm going to admit you to our obstetrics ward here for observation,' Lola told Maria as soon as Diego re-joined them, looking better if a little embarrassed. 'It's just a precaution but you took a nasty knock to the head.'

Maria looked as if she might protest, but one glance at Xavier and her husband silenced her.

'Thank you, Dr Garcia,' Diego said.

'Sir, if I could have your keys,' Xavier asked the

man, 'I'll move your vehicle to the car park.' He held out his hand and Diego handed the keys over.

Lola stepped out of the room with Xavier. 'Thank you again,' she said, squeezing his arm. 'I don't know what I would have done without you tonight and it's not over yet.'

His forearm tensed under her hand, his physical strength and warmth comforting.

'You're welcome, Dr Garcia.' He stepped back, putting some distance between them, as if her touch bothered him.

Momentarily taken aback by her body's violent reaction to his proximity and the warm earthy scent of his cologne, she dropped her arm to her side. But maybe because tonight was unlike any other night she'd known in the nine years she'd worked at the clinic, maybe because she'd seen another unexpected side to this man she responded to more than any man she'd met in years, she couldn't let it go.

'What's it going to take for you to call me Lola?' she pushed, suddenly desperate to hear her name on his lips now that she'd witnessed that killer smile of his.

He paused, turned and shrugged. 'Like you said, the night isn't over,' he said cryptically. 'And neither is the storm.'

She watched him walk away, a sigh of something like longing trapped in her throat. Xavier Torres was the kind of man who made a woman like her all too aware that there was more to life than work. Maybe there was more than one thing missing from her life, beyond professional challenge. But fixing that would need to wait. Xavier was right. There was more work to be done.

CHAPTER THREE

By half past midnight, an ominous calm had descended, at least indoors. Outside the hospital the storm raged on. The news reports cataloguing the extensive damage all across the island, to roads, trees, power lines and property.

Lola had just completed a round of the wards, checking in with each one, when she returned to her office and found Xavier waiting outside.

'I thought you probably hadn't eaten,' he said, holding out a plate of sandwiches and fruit covered with plastic wrap.

Lola took the offering with a groan of gratitude. 'Thank you. I'm starving. Have you eaten?' she asked, unlocking her office door, preceding him inside.

'The army taught us the importance of keeping energy levels up and staying hydrated,' he said in a non-answer.

She smiled at his seriousness. 'Well, they trained you well. Come in. I need an update.'

She washed her hands and sat on the sofa, inviting him to sit too. It seemed her office had become their unofficial storm command post. 'What's going on out there?' she asked. 'Anything I should know about?'

Peeling the plastic wrap from the plate, she invited him to share before helping herself to a bunch of grapes.

He declined with a shake of his head. 'I've eaten something, thanks.' Then he began his report. 'The government has declared a national state of emergency, effective from midnight. Civil defence have deployed the armed forces to assist in search and rescue, crisis management and temporary shelter for those who've had to abandon their homes due to flooding and other damage.'

Lola nodded for him to continue as she wiped her mouth with a napkin.

'Currently, there is no damage to the hospital's property, although I suspect the grounds will be a mess when all of this is over.'

Lola shrugged in agreement, selecting a sandwich while he went on.

'There have been no breaches of security to report,' he said. 'All of our communication systems are operative and maintenance say there's enough fuel to run the backup generators for a week, which hopefully won't be necessary.'

'Thanks, Xavier.' She sighed, leaning back against the cushions. 'I'm so glad you stayed to help. I really appreciate you.'

He jerked his chin in a small nod, then glanced at the TV screen on the wall. Lola had muted the sound earlier, but now she adjusted the volume so they could listen to the latest news update.

'Isolated reports of damage have been trickling in over the past few hours,' the newscaster said. 'Three people were injured when a tree fell on the vehicle they were travelling in. Flash flooding in the *Cazorla Valley* has inundated homes and farms, prompting emergency evacuations. And two fishermen and their boat are missing off the *Costa de las Estrellas*, search and rescue operations being severely hampered by four-metre swells.'

Muting the sound again, Lola retrieved two bottles of mineral water from the fridge and handed Xavier one. 'Have there been any more requests from St Sebastian's? I wonder how they're coping.'

'No, ma'am. One of my team, Antonio, the security guard on duty tonight, is married to a nurse who works in the emergency department there. I understand it's predictably busy.'

She sighed. 'It's at times like this when I wish I could do more to help.'

'You are helping. You're a doctor and you're needed here.'

'Yes,' she stated simply. 'I guess the storm has made me even more restless.' Something was missing from her life and, short of moving overseas to work for that medical relief charity, she had no idea how to figure out exactly what it was or how to fix it.

'Storms will do that,' he said. 'Do you...miss your family?'

At the mention of her loved ones, Lola smiled, astonished that she'd finally got him talking. 'I do. We're very close. Especially me and my twin sister, Isla. Do you have siblings?

'I'm an only child,' he said.

'I'm very lucky,' she said, 'especially as I see them often. My parents love Castilona. Mum is retired, apart from her charity work. Dad is a landscape artist so he takes inspiration from everywhere he travels and he always brings his sketchbook and paints when he visits.'

Xavier nodded. 'No shortage of stunning scenery around here. Let's hope the storm hasn't caused lasting damage to any of it.'

'Your country is beautiful. I guess that's why I'm still here. It will be hard to move away if I decide to change direction.'

'How long have you lived here?'

'Nine years. I worked at St Sebastian's after leaving medical school in Spain then took a job here. I became clinical director three years ago.'

'Is your mother a doctor, too?'

'No. I don't know where my career aspirations originated. I think it was from reading that series of famous books, *Medical Magic*, as a child.' She laughed softly, heartened when he smiled. 'What about you? Did you always want to be a soldier?'

A veil fell over his expression, tension returning to his mouth as if he disliked her question or didn't care to answer. 'Not really. But I grew up seeing quite a bit of palace life and state traditions, so it was a logical step for someone like me.'

'Someone like you? What does that mean?'

'Someone patriotic and free of family ties.' His eyes hardened a fraction, his posture stiffening. 'I was raised by a single mother. I never knew my father. Instead of going off the rails as a teen, I signed up to join the army.'

'And they taught you discipline and medical skills?'

'And most importantly self-respect.'

'I see,' she said, her voice a croak. The clinic's head of security had demons she could never fully understand. Maybe that was why he kept his feelings to himself and kept people at a distance. 'I understand from your employment records you were medically discharged.'

He sat a little taller. His voice, when he spoke again, devoid of emotion. 'I was injured in an explosion. I sustained a head injury and was knocked unconscious. When I woke up, I was diagnosed with a detached retina in one eye. I had surgery but it didn't help. The injury had gone too far.'

Lola nodded, instinctively knowing that would

have had a massive psychological impact on him. 'That must have been difficult for you. I'm sorry it happened,' she said. 'How does it affect you?'

He hesitated for a second, as if he didn't want to talk about it, but then he said, 'I have blurred vision and some peripheral visual field loss on that side. I compensate by turning my head to the affected side, but I've learned to adapt over the years. Fortunately, I'm still able to drive.'

'I see,' she said, instinct telling her the limitation would bother a man like him, especially given his work and personality. 'You don't like talking about yourself much, do you?'

'I don't know you,' he said.

'Which is why I'm asking questions. Tonight has been...unusual.'

'What else would you like to know?' he asked, his stare bold and unwavering, as if he knew the contents of her head.

'What makes you tick,' she said, raising her chin.

'I'm a simple man. What you see is what you get.'

'I very much doubt that.' She paused, instinct telling her that was only half his story. 'I think we all have hidden depths. Things we keep from people because we find them uncomfortable.'

'And what's yours?' he asked without missing a beat. Xavier didn't shy away from confrontation but, in deflecting, he'd cleverly avoided sharing *his* secret.

Lola took a deep breath, liking that he wasn't afraid to challenge her. She was being nosy and he'd turned the tables. 'I'm scared,' she said boldly. 'Scared that if I don't keep going, keep striving, I'll somehow lose myself.' As she'd almost done when she'd agreed to marry Nicolás.

He held her stare, a moment of honest connection between them. 'I think you know who you are and what you want.'

Lola stilled, her pulse bounding. His observation made her feel naked. Her attraction to him doubling. She *did* know what she wanted. She craved independence and professional success. But she was also a woman attracted to a man. *This* man.

'If that's all,' he said, standing. 'I'll continue my rounds.'

'Of course.' Lola stood too, disappointed that she'd confessed more than she'd learned. 'Perhaps when you've finished your rounds you should try to get some sleep.' As much as she enjoyed his company, it had been a long day so far.

'I'll be fine,' he said, securely in control of himself.

Just then, her phone rang and she jumped, the ring tone far too loud for this time of night. Snatching it up from the desk she answered.

'Dr Garcia,' someone said, 'Maria Fernandez,

the patient you admitted for observation following a head injury, is in labour. Her waters broke five minutes ago and she's already eight centimetres dilated.'

Lola's gaze flew to Xavier's. He'd stayed in the room, waiting and listening to her side of the conversation, presumably to offer help if required.

'I'm on my way,' Lola said, hanging up the phone. 'Ever delivered a baby?' she asked him in answer to his questioning look.

'I have actually, once,' he said shrugging, unconcerned by the prospect of helping.

'Good. The last babies I helped to bring into the world were the royal princes. But that was in an assisting capacity with a world leading obstetrics expert leading the procedure and in a fully equipped theatre. I'd appreciate your calming influence,' she told him, reaching for her stethoscope.

'Then I'm all yours,' he said, filling her with confidence, and together they headed for the obstetrics ward.

'And here's your baby,' Lola said from behind her mask as she raised the newborn girl into her mother's waiting arms.

Xavier swallowed, a lump in his throat the size of a football. That the delivery had gone without a hitch, tonight of all nights when there was only a skeleton staff on the obstetrics ward given there hadn't been any planned deliveries, was testament to Lola's amazing skills as a physician. She was incredibly talented. He felt…euphoric that the delivery had gone so smoothly, so he could only imagine how the parents felt.

For a moment, Lola glanced up and met his stare, her eyes crinkled in the corners so he knew she was smiling in gratitude. But all he'd done was hold Maria's hand opposite her husband and observe the foetal heart rate monitor for signs of distress as Lola had instructed.

He smiled back, wishing he could tell her 'well done', not that she needed his praise. But the more time he spent with her, the keener he was to get away. She was slowly wheedling her way under his ever-present guard. Pushing to get to know him. Sharing parts of herself as easily as she shared her smile and her compliments. It was messing with his head, making him imagine things he shouldn't. Making him want things he didn't need, like connection.

With his hand holding duties complete, Xavier stepped away from the bedside, allowing Maria and Diego time to bond with their tiny daughter. He moved towards the door, shutting down the pointless emotions the delivery of a baby had stirred up. He'd often dreamed of fatherhood, but every time the thought popped into his head, he shut it quickly down. Firstly, he'd never had a relationship serious enough to warrant the dream and secondly, he never wanted to be like his own father—an absent, self-serving, narcissist. The only thing his mother had ever told him about the man was that he hadn't wanted to be involved.

Xavier paused at the door. Lola and the midwife were busy, and while the unexpected arrival of baby Fernandez made this a night Xavier would always remember, he didn't really belong there. Truth was, he wasn't sure where he belonged. Never had been. But he'd made his peace with that long ago. No point wishing for something he'd never had. Better to do everything in his power to make his life secure. And now that he was thirty-five, he certainly had no need for a father. Especially not one who would callously abandon and reject his own son.

He was just about to leave the room and get back to work when the lights flickered out. Everyone froze for a second.

'Don't worry,' he said. 'There must be a power cut. The generator will take over soon.'

Sure enough, in the next second, the lights flickered back on and Lola shot him another of those grateful looks over her shoulder. A man like him could get used to the way she looked at him. As if he was something special. But tonight was just one of those nights. The storm creating an artificial environment where it was easy to believe that normal rules failed to apply.

But his rules kept him safe and in control of his

own existence. His support network, the people he allowed close, was small. Except Lola's gentle questions, and the chemistry that had become glaringly obvious was mutual, kept nudging him just out of his comfort zone.

'I'll check in with maintenance,' he told Lola, removing his mask and apron, determined to keep his head around this woman, who was after all, his boss. Just because tonight had thrown them together, didn't mean he should act on the attraction he'd been struggling to ignore since the first day they'd met.

'Can you do a circuit of the wards, too?' she asked him. 'Make sure all vital equipment is functioning properly. See if they need anything while I finish up here.'

'Of course,' he said, glad to have a reason to distance himself from her as he set off on his rounds. It had been a pretty intense night so far and it wasn't over. Lola Garcia had a kind of freaky intuition. As if she knew human nature and could see right through him, see that deep inside him there would always be a fear that his father had left because Xavier was lacking somehow. He didn't want her to see those dark places in him. He'd spent most of his adult life keeping people out emotionally. There was no reason to change that now, no matter how amazing and sexy the hospital's clinical director was.

CHAPTER FOUR

THIRTY MINUTES LATER, after a shower and a change of clothes into a clean uniform he kept in his locker, his head was clearer.

Storms often made people behave out of character. Unless Lola specifically called for his help he would steer clear of her for the rest of the night. No more food deliveries simply because he recognised how hard she worked and how she put everyone around her first. No more personal chats where he allowed himself to be lured by her openness into sharing more than he normally would. No more enjoying her lingering looks of appreciation and gratitude. It was time to claw back some distance.

He'd just secured his locker in the staff quarters—a central communal lounge and a fully equipped kitchen, surrounded by a series of ensuite bedrooms for staff to sleep if working overnight—when there was a knock at the main door.

Wondering if Antonio had lost his key pass, he pulled open the door to find Lola on the threshold.

She'd changed too. She wore a set of the clinic's navy blue scrubs and her hair was pulled back into a neat ponytail, the ends damp as if she too had showered after the delivery of baby Fernandez.

'Dr Garcia,' he said, shocked, his manners deserting him as he kept her on the threshold and tried not to gaze at her body, which was killer—even in the scrubs. He'd never once seen her in the staff quarters. 'Is everything okay?'

He checked the walkie talkie he kept on his belt, worried he'd missed a call. But the charge light was green showing the device was in full working order.

'I just wanted to check on you,' she said looking up at him with a smile, her straight white teeth scraping at her plump lower lip. 'That all happened rather quickly and then with the power going out… You left in a hurry. Are you okay? Not too traumatised by the birth?'

'I'm fine,' Xavier said automatically, trying to recall the last time someone other than his mother had worried about his welfare or state of mind and coming up blank.

His personal relationships were always casual. The last woman he'd slept with was some aide to a visiting ambassador who had made it perfectly clear that all she'd wanted from him was an orgasm or two. And that had suited him just fine. He'd been too focussed on building a career and a comfortable life for himself to chase love and commitment. Which, unlike security and knowing who he could trust, were things he could do without.

'Thanks for asking,' he said, clearing his throat. 'How's the...um, little one doing?'

What was wrong with him? Was he starstruck by Lola because she was good at her job? Her position as his boss had forced him to ignore their chemistry these past six months. But if they'd met under different circumstances, if he'd acted on his attraction, it might be out of his system by now.

'She's good.' Lola smiled again and leaned against the door jamb, obviously in no hurry to leave. 'A little small, but that's normal for her gestation. So tell me about the baby you delivered.'

'I was deployed overseas with the army,' Xavier said. 'My unit came across what we assumed was a deserted building until we heard moans. I went in to search and found a local woman labouring alone.'

'So you helped her? Just you?' Her stare shone with admiration.

'She did all the work,' he said. 'I simply stayed and provided an extra pair of hands when it came to catching the baby and dealing with the umbilical cord. Then we transported them both to the hospital.'

'Wow. That's...impressive.'

'Apologies,' he said, stepping back and swinging the door wide, finally recalling his manners. 'Would you like to come in? There's no one else here, but there's a kitchen. Tea and coffee. Snacks in the cupboard.'

The last thing he needed was any more of her company. Lola Garcia, while insanely hot, already saw him far too clearly for comfort. But still, he found himself hoping she'd accept the invitation.

'Thanks.' She nodded and stepped into the room, glancing around. The staff quarters, like the rest of the clinic, were comfortable bordering on luxurious compared to some accommodations he'd seen.

'Do you have any Marcona almonds?' she asked referring to the gourmet Spanish snack, her eyes bright with excitement as she bypassed the lounge and headed for the kitchen. 'I have a soft spot for those as they remind me of home.'

'Let's find out,' he said, pulling open cupboards and drawers to reveal an array of options. Maybe if they found the snack, she'd leave and he could set about forgetting the way she looked at him as if she *did* indeed know what she wanted and knew only he could give it to her.

Peering over his shoulder, she stepped so close he was bathed in the scent of her shampoo and something else—the warm natural fragrance of her skin.

For a terrifying second, he feared he might forget himself and dip his face to the side of her neck, inhale that honey scent that had been plaguing him all night long as they'd worked together, then kiss her skin. It had clearly been too long since he'd been with a woman.

'There they are,' he said, having spied the almonds near the back of the drawer. He reached for them and almost wept for joy.

At the exact same moment, Lola squealed with delight and did the same. Their hands collided. He froze, tensing every muscle in his body while desire hot and insistent ransacked him. When you worked security, stillness was your friend. The human gaze was naturally drawn to movement. And if ever there was a moment he needed to be invisible, it was now. Otherwise, she might look at him with another impassioned look. He might drag her into his arms and taste those soft, pouty lips. Test whether she'd taste as good as he imagined. Drag out a moan from her cultured mouth.

Beside him, Lola gasped and withdrew her hand as if she'd been burned by his touch. Her stare flew to his. Her pupils dilated. Her breathing shallow and fast.

Swallowing discreetly, he held out the bag of almonds to her. It wasn't too late to gloss over that accidental touch that had awoken every nerve ending in his body. He could pretend it hadn't happened, pretend they were both oblivious to the hair-raising crackle of sexual awareness and the warm scented cloud of pheromones engulfing them.

But she hadn't stepped away. If anything, she appeared to have leaned closer.

She blinked up at him. 'Thanks,' she said. Her fingers closed around the snack held between them. Neither one pulling away as the seconds stretched and Xavier's mind blanked to all the reasons kissing her would be a bad idea.

He stared, willing her to take the almonds and leave. No good would come from the way she was looking at him. As if she too wanted a couple of orgasms and nothing more. But maybe because of the intense and unexpected events of the night, they seemed bound by a new kind of understanding. As if here and now, for this single moment in time, they were just a man and woman. Insanely attracted to each other. No boundaries. No differences. No expectations.

Xavier waited. A primal instinct building inside him. Urging him to act on the impulses he'd experienced every day since first meeting her. He wanted to know if she'd moan when he kissed her. If her skin would feel as good as it smelled. If, when he pushed inside her, she'd gasp his name.

'You should go,' he said, dragging the words from some disciplined corner of his mind that was still in control. He didn't need her acceptance. What he wanted from her was far more animalistic. Would the sophisticated doctor be shocked if she could read his mind?

Expecting her to nod, to agree or move away, he braced himself for the loss of her body warmth, the soft rasp of her breath, the way her pupils swallowed almost all of her amber streaked irises. But as much as he would regret her absence, he wanted her gone before he did something stupid. She was his boss. A woman who frequented the world of wealth and privilege. A world he'd been around his entire life but to which he could never belong and that was fine by him. Finally, in his thirties, he knew who he was—even if he only understood half of his heritage.

'I hate being told what to do,' she said softly, her tongue swiping her bottom lip as her gaze dropped to his mouth and he knew instantly that they *would* kiss. It seemed inevitable. An unspoken agreement.

'Then do what you want,' he said, certain that this independent and driven woman had always made her own destiny. Something he could relate to and something he found so attractive.

She stared for a handful of seconds, her breasts rising and falling with every breath. Then she tugged the almonds from his grasp and tossed them carelessly onto the counter.

Before she could step closer—he'd read her intent in the lowering of her eyelids, the half-step she began in his direction, the start of a soft moan at the back of her throat—he gripped her face between his palms and covered her mouth with his. Tasting those lush lips, parting them. Touching the tip of his tongue to hers when she offered it and it sliding deeper into her mouth as her hands, rested on his chest, curled into his shirt.

She moaned. A low, needy sound that lured him deeper into madness. He'd been right. She tasted fantastic and she wanted this too. Wanted him. As reckless as it was, he couldn't stop himself from indulging, just for a second, in the passion of their heated kiss. Growing more determined, she surged up on to the balls of her feet and pressed her gorgeous body to his. Her breasts against his chest. Her stomach aligned with his groin where his erection stirred. Her hands gripping his shoulders and tugging him closer.

'Xavier,' she said, dropping her head back, her eyes closed. Her hands raked his back, her fingers curling into the belt loops on his trousers to hold their bodies flush as if she couldn't quite get close enough. But Xavier had discipline in spades.

'Tell me what you want from this,' he said, unable to stop himself from sliding his lips over the soft skin below her ear where her natural scent was strongest and then down the side of her neck so she moaned again, those full lips parted. He wasn't anyone's for ever and he needed her to understand that.

'I want you,' she said on a sigh, her eyes still

closed as he tunnelled his hands into her hair and angled her head to give himself better access to her neck. Her body pressed to his was driving him wild. 'Just one time,' she added. 'No strings.'

A groan rumbled inside his head. She was perfect and so sexy. He was struggling to think of anything beyond that condom he always kept in his wallet.

'You sure?' he asked, one arm around her waist holding her close. His other hand cupped her breast so he could thumb the nipple that peeked through her clothes as if begging for his touch. 'Because I only do casual. I'm not the romance type.'

Love was all about belonging and he'd made himself content to emotionally drift.

'Yes,' she said, emphatic. Her body writhed restlessly against his. Her hand slipped between them to rub at his erection. 'I only do casual too. I value my work and my independence too much for anything else.'

He kissed her again and her eyes drifted closed, a dreamy look on her face as he stroked her nipple, as if she'd been fantasising about this every bit as much as him. But if they were doing this, he needed her to be certain. He worked his hand underneath her scrub top to where the lace of her bra cupped her flesh and pulled back from her lips.

'Lola, open your eyes,' he said.

At this command, the sound of her name on his

lips, she did just that, looking up at him with such heated desire he almost groaned aloud at how royally screwed he was. Now that he'd kissed her, tasted those soft lips, heard those breathy moans he'd fantasised about and learned the shape of her curves, his resistance was crumbling fast.

Still he clung to the last shred. 'Normally, I'd point out that this is a terrible idea. We work together. You're my boss.' His arm flexed around her waist, bringing her closer so the heat and softness of her body melded to him.

'It's hardly a normal night,' she challenged. 'And I know what I want.'

Because her stroking was driving him to distraction, he dived for her lips once more. Her tongue surged against his. Her hands sliding inside his shirt. Her nails lightly scraping his back, urging him on.

Certain that they wouldn't be interrupted, he gripped her waist and sat her on the kitchen counter. 'I need to see you,' he said, standing between her spread thighs while he raised the scrub top over her head, casting it aside impatiently.

Her breasts were perfect pale, creamy mounds encased in a sexy black lace bra. He filled his hands with them, his thumbs rubbing over the nipples so she gasped and scraped her teeth over that bottom lip again as she watched, thrusting her chest forward into his touch.

He kissed her again, popping the clasp on her

bra so he could remove it. Her breasts filled his hands perfectly, her nipples hard and responsive as she moaned louder and tugged at the hem of his shirt.

She threw his shirt to the floor and ran her hands and eyes over his chest and shoulders, pressing her warm skin to his so he feared he might combust.

'Hold tight,' he said as she wrapped her arms around his neck and he scooped her from the counter, carrying her with her legs around his waist as he made for his room.

The staff bedrooms were designed for sleep—sparsely furnished with a king single bed, nightstand and small closet. But Lola didn't seem to care about the room's minimalist functionality. The minute he laid her down against the clean bed linen, she tugged eagerly at his neck and brought him down on top of her.

'Hurry, I want you,' she said, shoving the waistband of her scrub trousers over her hips.

Xavier extricated himself from her wild kisses. He took one nipple in his mouth, smiling when she sighed and speared her fingers through his hair, holding him in place, moaning his name, demanding more.

He took his wallet from his pocket and removed the condom. They each removed their trousers and underwear so they were completely naked, tossing everything in a pile on the floor. Xavier knelt between her bent legs on the bed. His gaze scouring every inch of her glorious body. His hands gliding along her thighs and hips up her ribs to cup her breasts.

She sat up, her arms around his back, and pressed kisses and swipes of the tip of her tongue to his chest and abs. Dipping lower and lower. He closed his eyes for a second, burned alive by the passion of her touch. Then her hand encircled his erection and she took him in her mouth. His eyes suddenly opened. His jaw clenched hard against the intensity of the pleasure.

'Lola...' Her name came easily now, no deference required. Here, like this with naked need the only thing between them, they were equals in every way.

She looked up at him and smiled. He pulled back, grabbed the condom and slid it on, too impatient to enjoy her mouth on him any longer.

She pushed him back into a sitting position against the wall and straddled his lap, gripping his shoulders as she slowly lowered herself onto him. Her lip snagged beneath her teeth and her eyes locked to his so he saw the desire and determination there. Was there any sight sexier than a woman who knew what she wanted and wasn't afraid to chase it?

Xavier gripped her hips, controlling her descent

and the depth of his penetration. She gasped and moaned his name as he filled her.

'You feel so good,' she whispered against his ear.

He crushed her to his chest, his arms banded around her back, his face buried between her breasts as he forgot to breathe in the face of such powerful pleasure. Lola tunnelled her fingers through his hair, cradled his head and began to move. Rocking her hips, driving him wild, sending licks of flame streaking from his groin to his gut and down his legs.

Her moans intensified as he caressed her buttocks and directed the speed of her rocking hips to a rhythm that sent stars sparking behind his eyes. She might have been made for him, so tight was her grip on him. So attuned were their movements. Their desire for each other so in sync.

Needing more friction, needing her untamed, he gripped her thighs and flipped her onto her back in one deft move, still buried deep inside her. She gasped, her mouth open, her stare on his as he took over. His shallow thrusts growing deeper and faster, riding them both hard as she gripped his arms like he was the only thing grounding her to Earth.

'Xavier,' she cried, her breath catching. Her breasts bouncing enticingly.

He kissed her deep. His tongue duelling with hers as his entire body stretched taut, braced for the explosion and the euphoria that lay just out of reach. She engulfed him. Her tight heat agonising torture. Her scent clinging to his skin so he'd smell her long after this was over. Her taste as addictive as the sounds of her unrestrained desire.

Tearing his mouth from hers he dived for her nipple, sucking it into his mouth. Flicking the tip of his tongue over the bud as he raised her thigh over his hip and thrust faster, deeper, harder until she cried out in ecstasy. Her elegantly manicured fingernails dug into his shoulders as her orgasm struck and he let go, joining her in the moment of ecstasy.

With a harsh groan he couldn't hold inside, he surrendered. His body rigid as he came. His head full of the sound of her fading cries and panting breaths as they clung to each other until every last drop of pleasure was spent.

CHAPTER FIVE

A WEEK LATER, Lola bade farewell to Castilona's royal family after their visit to the clinic. The baby twins, Princes Rafael and Rodrigo, had passed their six-month health check with flying colours.

'Xavier will accompany you to the car park, Your Majesty,' she told King Octavio, a handsome and imposing man clearly besotted with his queen, Phoebe, and his adorable sons.

'Thank you, Dr Garcia,' he replied, warmly shaking her hand. 'For everything.'

Queen Phoebe added her thanks and the family, accompanied by their own team of security and not one but two royal nannies, stepped into the private elevator that would take them directly to the secure underground car park so they could leave the hospital unobserved.

Before the elevator doors closed, Lola glanced at Xavier, their eyes meeting. Her breath halted. A delicious shudder quivered in her stomach as it had done every time their eyes met since *that* intense but incredible night.

Thanks to the storm, Lola's normal workload had increased. What with minor repairs, and the clean-up of the hospital's grounds, there'd been no time for a private conversation with Xavier. In fact, as agreed, they'd kept their distance from one another, acting as if the intimacies of that night hadn't happened.

The lift doors closed and Lola released the breath she'd been holding, her mind ensnared by the exquisite memories. She'd never known passion like it. After the first time, they'd showered together and he'd gone down on her in the cubicle, one thigh over his shoulder, his hands gripping her backside and the water pounding them both. If he hadn't held her upright as he groaned out his encouragement, she'd have collapsed to the tiles so astounding was her second orgasm.

After she'd returned the favour to him, glorying in how thoroughly she'd reduced such a tall and powerful man to a shattered wreck, they'd dressed in silence and then agreed to put that night behind them and resume their cordial working relationship.

Now, Lola returned to her office on shaky legs. Standing at her desk, she'd just opened her emails when she spied Xavier across the main foyer having returned from the car park. He strode across the marbled tiles, headed her way. Every step he took shunting her pulse higher, as if her body recognised and anticipated the source of such incredible pleasure. Heat flooded her system, centred most insistently between her legs.

She straightened her spine and tried to shut down the memories of him holding her so close she thought she might not be able to breathe. Of him moving inside her, desire darkening his stare to almost black. Of the expression of sheer determination on his face as he'd looked up at her in the shower, his tongue and clever fingers thrusting her once more into oblivion.

'Come in,' she said, when he reached the open door. 'Did their departure go to plan? Without incident?' Her voice cracked and she prayed he hadn't heard it.

'Yes, ma'am. The wolves have left the den,' he said using the code name supplied by the palace security team. He stood erect, feet spread, arms clasped behind his back, reminding Lola that despite that incredible night, they'd agreed to resume business as usual.

Except every time he addressed her as ma'am, or Dr Garcia, all she heard was him groaning *Lola*.

Closing the door, she sat on the edge of her desk facing him, her eyes meeting his. 'Good. I wanted to touch base now that things have returned to normal after Gabriel,' she said, although the cyclone had ravaged the island, leaving considerable damage in its wake. 'We haven't worked together much this week.'

'I've been on night shifts,' he confirmed, clearly back to his restrained self. All evidence of that torrid passion concealed.

She nodded, wishing he'd look at her the way he had that night. As if he hadn't been able to stop himself from wanting her, no matter how hard he'd tried. But she needed to follow his example. To put all that from her mind and act professionally. After all, she was his boss at least for the next few weeks. She'd finally got around to sending that resignation email that morning, setting the wheels of her departure from *Clinico San Carlos*, and from Castilona, in motion.

'So we're good?' she asked, hesitantly. 'You and I, I mean?' Her breathing sped up, an itch of frustration spreading over her skin because he was still staring at the window over her shoulder.

He glanced her way then. His expression bland. His dark stare unreadable. 'We're good, Dr Garcia.'

Lola concealed her sigh. She was being unreasonable and selfish wanting more than his usual polite competence. She wanted to see his fire. His abandon. That glorious moment when his restraint had snapped and he'd dragged her into his arms, kissing her with such ferocious need that she'd instantly known he'd been smothering his attraction for her since the day they'd met.

'Good,' she said instead as she stood and took her seat behind the desk. 'One more thing, I wanted to let you know that I've handed in my resignation.'

A frown slashed his brows. 'Why? I hope it's nothing to do with...that night.'

Ignoring the regret she'd probably imagined in his eyes, she rushed to reassure him. 'No, no. I've been thinking of it for a while. The board will, I'm sure, accept my resignation. If they have any sense, they'll appoint Dr Lomas to the position of clinical director. But whomever they appoint, I'm sure that you and all the other staff will find the transition a smooth one.'

A few beats of awkward silence passed during which she wished she could tell what he was thinking. But Xavier was clearly practised at keeping people out. He might have momentarily lowered his guard and slept with her, but it seemed they weren't going to be friends.

'Where do you plan to go?' he asked, showing no indication that he cared one way or another.

And that was fine. They'd shared an amazing night and neither of them wanted more. Except for a brief moment afterwards, as she'd tried to put herself back together, that restlessness she'd been experiencing had lessened.

'I've ended my tenancy on my home here,' she said. 'I'll go back to Spain in the first instance. Then...well, we'll see. Maybe overseas for a while.'

She didn't have all the details figured out yet,

but she'd been looking at medical aid charities, or maybe considering pursuing a master's degree.

Xavier nodded. 'Then I wish you well, Dr Garcia.'

'Thank you.' She looked up to find his stare was trained on the window once more. The matter, what they'd meant to one another that night, resolved. 'I'll let you get back to work.'

He nodded and left. And just like that, their connection, be it real or imagined, seemed severed.

Three weeks later

Xavier knocked at the back door of his mother's cottage and entered her warm and fragrant kitchen. After weeks of trying to forget that night with Lola, of shoving aside unsettling thoughts of her impending departure for Spain, he finally had another thing on which to focus—the contents of the disturbing letter clutched in his tight fist.

'Not working today?' Carlota asked on spying him. She dusted her floury hands on her apron and greeted him with a warm embrace before she resumed kneading dough for her *telera*, the Andalusian white bread she'd baked for him every day of his childhood and beyond.

'I've taken the week off,' he said, dragging in a patient breath laced with the sweet smell of baking, for which he had zero appetite. 'I need you to explain this to me, Mamá.'

Keeping a grip on his temper, he placed the letter on the counter, his mind still spinning at its unbelievable contents.

Carlota Torres read the letter, her hand steady at first, but then trembling as her eyes scanned the page. Xavier's stomach knotted tighter. Her shocked reaction, the flush of shame on her cheeks, all the confirmation he needed that the letter's claims were genuine.

She met his stare, her hand covering her mouth. 'I'm so sorry. I wanted to tell you. I almost did, a million times.'

'So it's true?' he asked, his mind rebelling because he'd spent his entire life wondering where he'd come from, who he was related to, and all this time the answer had been there in front of his face.

Carlota sank into a kitchen chair and looked up pleadingly. 'I was young. He was handsome and charming back then,' she said about Mauricio de la Rosa, the King's uncle, a man Xavier had feared growing up because he'd never witnessed anything other than a disappointed scowl from him.

Tears slid down Carlota's cheeks. He crouched before her, gently taking her hands in a silent plea. He hated to see her cry. He wanted answers, not to upset her. But with a secret of this magnitude, he guessed upset was inevitable.

'He seduced me,' she said. 'And I was flattered. I didn't know until it was too late that he was already engaged to someone—Xiomara's mother.' She cupped his face lovingly, the way she'd always done, as if Xavier was her pride and joy. 'When I found out you were coming, I went to him and told him. I'd never seen him angry until that moment when he finally showed me his ruthless side.'

Xavier swore under his breath, positive that if the hateful man hadn't already died from a stroke three weeks ago, as he had according to the letter, he would have personally hunted him down and throttled him for his treatment of Carlota.

'He wanted to…fix the problem—' she said, tremulously, '—but I refused. I wanted you. I told him I'd raise you alone. That was when he persuaded me that it was in your best interests to never know who your father was.' She gripped Xavier's hands tighter, as if begging him to understand. 'He said if the world knew the scandal, you'd be a target. You'd never be able to live a normal life. You'd be hounded by the media. You might even be at risk of harm, given his status.'

Confused and reeling, Xavier shook his head. 'You should have told me anyway, when I was old enough to understand.' He hated what she'd endured, but he'd spent all those years wondering.

What difference might it have made to his life if he'd known the truth?

Carlota nodded, swiping aside her tears. 'I should. But by then I was ashamed that I'd ever fallen for the charms of someone so poisonous. He'd matured into the selfish, power hungry and cruel regent.' She held his stare, her eyes hard. 'You are *nothing* like him. Nothing. I didn't want you to think for one second that you were.'

Xavier stood and collapsed into the seat facing hers. How many nights had he slept in this house, wondering about the man who should have been there to guide and raise him when all along that man had known of his existence, had practically watched him grow and had still chosen to disown him?

Reaching for his hand, his mother, leaned close. 'I should have told you. You're right. But I wanted to keep you safe. From his world and from him. You saw what he was. How he treated people. Even his own daughter.'

Xavier sucked in a breath. Princess Xiomara. Technically, this news made her his half-sister... No, having worked for her for years he couldn't think of her that way.

'So why didn't you move us away?' he asked, confused and nauseous, the full implications dawning on him. Would the princess accept this news, or reject him too? He liked and respected her, but theirs had always been a transactional relationship. One where it had been his job to protect her.

'With you on the way, I needed the money,' Carlota said, raising her chin in determination. 'This job was secure, well-paid and it came with this house for life. Besides, Mauricio didn't live at the palace until years later. After his brother died. By then you were in the army. A grown man. He'd never shown the slightest interest in you, so I figured he would leave you alone. Which thankfully he did.'

'Until now,' Xavier said bitterly, pointing at the letter she'd discarded, which had arrived from a Spanish law firm and contained the details of his heritage, including the results of a paternity test and the inheritance left to him by a man who'd ignored him his whole life. Casa Colina was a hundred acre vineyard estate that came with an aristocratic title of *Marqués de Moro*.

'What will you do?' his mother asked hesitantly.

'With his estate? The title? The money?' He shrugged, furious, certain that de la Rosa's gift was intended to cause pain and havoc. 'Reject it…' The way his so-called father had rejected both his mother and him, not that he wanted to emulate such a hateful man. Carlota was right there.

She glanced at the letter. 'Who's been running things since Mauricio fled to Spain?' she asked quietly as if she was thinking about the jobs and welfare of the estate's employees, who numbered over sixty.

'I understand there's an estate manager in charge,' he said, already feeling the weight of the responsibility that had been thrust upon him. 'I'll find out the situation, then make some decisions.'

Carlota nodded, touching his arm. 'I know you will do what's right. You always have, which is how I know you are one hundred percent mine, as you have always been.' Her eyes blazed as she looked at him and just like every other day of his life, he felt her unconditional love and strength.

For an unguarded moment, Xavier closed his eyes on a wave of grief. But it was for a man that had never existed, apart from in his childhood imaginings. The reality of his father was nowhere close to those imaginings. The man had been totally unworthy of this kind, loyal, hard-working woman who'd raised Xavier alone while he'd lived a life of privilege.

'I'll leave you to your bread,' he said, hugging his mother goodbye. He needed time to think, to assimilate what he'd learned and figure out who he was in the face of this new information.

Before she released him, she gripped his face in her floury hands. 'I love you, my son.'

He nodded. 'Love you too, Mamá.'

That would never change. Even if, with the arrival of that letter, everything else in his life had.

CHAPTER SIX

ON HER FIRST Saturday off since the storm, and blind to the half-packed boxes cluttering up her entire apartment, Lola forced herself to catch up on some much needed life admin. The most pressing of which was her late period.

She wasn't religiously regular and she and Xavier had used a condom, so she fully expected the test she'd purchased that morning to be negative. But she preferred to have it confirmed over wasting time wondering and worrying.

She stared at the blue plastic stick on her bathroom vanity unit, trying to stay calm while she awaited the result. Logically the chances of her being pregnant were slim. She wasn't on birth control—she hadn't dated for two years—and she and Xavier had certainly put that one condom through its paces. But they'd been safe.

Thinking over the past few weeks, Lola paced to the bedroom, a ball of restless energy making her limbs jittery and her head full of pressure. She and Xavier had barely seen each other since she'd told him she was leaving. She'd been busy with the extra workload pertaining to the storm damage and her resignation, and he'd taken some annual leave, so she was unlikely to see him for a while longer. But the lack of interaction was a good thing. Helping Lola to move on from that night, even if she was still struggling to forget.

Pacing back to the bathroom, Lola glanced at the stick. Her hand flew to cover her mouth as she read the word in the window, which was clear and undeniable—*pregnant*.

Her other hand automatically dropped to her stomach, resting there protectively as a deluge of emotions washed through her—shock and disbelief uppermost. She was pregnant. With Xavier's baby.

Collapsing onto the edge of her bed she sniffed away the choked feeling in her throat as she thought about the tiny life growing inside her. She'd always wanted a child one day. She'd imagined it would be with a man she'd fallen in love with. A man who wanted her for the person she was. Not for how she might slot into his life, like Nicolás.

But this, she and Xavier, was an entirely different situation. They weren't in love. They weren't even a couple. He'd even dodged her attempts to get to know him on a deeper level. The only real thing she knew about him, besides his employment history and a bit about his past, was his prowess as a lover.

But this was happening and her first instinct was to call Isla, her twin sister.

'*Cómo estás?*' Isla answered, in her usual cheerful voice.

'I'm not sure...' Lola replied, swallowing. 'I... I've just discovered that I'm pregnant.' They were as close as it was possible to be so she didn't bother building up to the news.

'What?' Shocked silence followed Isla's question.

Lola wished she was there with her sister, in Spain, where she could seek the comfort of a hug.

'I know.' Lola scrunched her eyes closed, her face warm with embarrassment. She was a mature professional woman. A doctor. How could she have let this happen?

'I didn't know you were seeing anyone,' Isla said, warily.

'I'm not. It was a one night thing. Remember that cyclone we had...?'

'Ah...blame it on the storm.' There was no judgement in Isla's voice and Lola laughed mirthlessly.

'So what are you going to do?' Isla asked carefully.

Lola rubbed at her temple. 'I don't know. Have a baby I guess.' She was still in shock but already felt better having confided in her sister.

'Well, I'll be here to help you, not that you'll need it,' Isla said offering the kind of unconditional support that brought tears to Lola's eyes.

'Thanks, *manita*.' Suddenly ferociously homesick, Lola pressed the phone closer to her ear, wishing Isla was there.

'Have you told the father?' Isla asked.

Lola's stomach dropped. Xavier... How would he react? Would he want to be involved in their baby's life, or would she be doing this alone? It didn't matter. As a financially independent woman, she didn't need his input. But she owed it to him to tell him all the same. Could she stand to wait until he returned to work?

'No. But I will.' Maybe she should do it today. Get it over with so that in the few weeks she had left in Castilona, before she visited her family in Spain, they could come to some sort of arrangement.

Realising that the job with a charity organisation that serviced refugee camps, providing humanitarian aid, emergency health care and immunisation clinics, she'd applied for might no longer be suitable for a pregnant woman, she paced nervously.

'I need to go,' she told Isla.

Ever the pragmatist, she preferred action over contemplation. Better to tell Xavier right away, then she could figure everything else out.

She finished her phone call, then with a trembling hand, she dialled the number she had for Xavier, but it went to voicemail. Maybe he'd gone overseas on holiday. Logging into her work computer, she brought up his file and checked that the number was current. Then, because she preferred to have her answers today over tomorrow, Lola typed his address into the GPS app on her phone, grabbed her car keys from the bowl on the marble topped table in her hallway and headed for her car.

She might be in shock, but she was going to have this baby regardless of the timing. The sooner she informed Xavier, the sooner she'd know if he wanted to be involved or not and the sooner she could formulate a new plan.

Following the directions to the address from his file, she drove along the coastal road that clung to the side of the steep cliffs like a swag of ribbon on a Christmas tree. Slowly ascending the hill where the honey-coloured stone and terracotta rooftops of Castilona's hillside homes became more expansive. The million-euro views more and more breathtaking.

Near the top of the road, just before it flattened out to begin its descent down the other side, Lola pulled the car onto the indicated driveway. On the pavement opposite, a small group of photographers loitered, their cameras pop, pop, popping as they pointlessly recorded her arrival. There was nothing newsworthy about her, but her trepidation increased. Perhaps Xavier was living there with some sort of celebrity.

Confused by the grand ornate wrought iron gates blocking the drive, she lowered her window and pressed a button on the intercom box on the wall.

'*Hola,*' a female voice said. 'Welcome to Casa Colina.'

'My name is Lola Garcia. I'm looking for Xavier Torres,' Lola said hesitantly, wondering if she'd made a mistake. 'Do I have the correct address?' Maybe she'd typed it in incorrectly.

'*Sí,*' the woman replied. Seconds later, the gates swung open.

With her heart pounding, Lola followed the winding, tree-lined drive until a stunning sprawling villa came into view. Sitting atop the hill, the building had an almost three hundred and sixty degree view of the ocean, which from up here looked dyed turquoise as if someone had washed out paint from a giant paintbrush there.

Lola parked and exited her car, taking a moment to appreciate the beauty of the expansive, creamy stone villa, which was surrounded by terraces—some tiled for outdoor seating, some boasting manicured Mediterranean gardens and one composed entirely of an exquisite infinity pool that ran the length of the house.

A crunch of gravel sounded. Lola spun on her heel to find Xavier a few feet away. He was casually dressed in worn ripped jeans and a grey marl t-shirt. His strong square jaw covered in sexy scruff, his dark hair ruffled and his eyes wary.

'Lola,' he said, a small frown pinching his brows together and tugging down his lovely mouth. A mouth she could still taste if she didn't take care to concentrate on stifling those memories.

'You…haven't been at work,' she said, her voice accusing despite the real reason she was there.

'No. Would you like to come in?' he asked, looking far from comfortable as he slipped his hands into the back pockets of his jeans so his biceps flexed. She remembered exactly how it felt to be held in those strong arms. To feel his weight on top of her and the tenderness with which he'd cupped her face for the last time that night and brushed a goodbye kiss over her lips.

She hesitated, wishing she'd simply continued to call. After all, a woman had answered the intercom. Perhaps he was involved with someone now. Perhaps they lived in this stunning house together. Perhaps Lola was about to ruin his day and that of his new woman in his life with her news.

'I don't want to intrude…' she said, more uncertain of him in this environment because whenever she thought of his private life, she'd never pictured him living in a home like this.

'You're not,' he said. 'Come inside.'

Without waiting for her to ask any more questions he turned and led the way to a side entrance that after a few turns down cool, dim, stone flagged corridors, led into a sun bathed kitchen.

'Would you like something to drink?' he asked, leaning against the counter, his hands curled over the edge besides his hip as if he felt both at home and uncomfortable.

'No, thank you,' she said, embarrassed that his unease might be due to her just turning up out of the blue when they'd agreed to move on. 'I won't intrude for long. Is…is this *your* house?' she asked, his reticence irking her and making her paranoid. 'It's breathtaking.'

But he needn't worry. She hadn't come to beg for more sex or suggest they date. Of course, she was also stalling. But maybe because she'd once rejected a life of wealth and privilege as Nicolás's wife, she just couldn't picture Xavier living here. It was throwing her off, shoving the very important reason she'd come aside.

'Yes,' he stated simply.

'I don't understand,' she said, glancing around the state of the art designer kitchen that definitely possessed a woman's touch—a giant vase of Hydrangeas on the island counter, a soft throw draped over the sofa in the adjoining conservatory where tropical house-plants and culinary herbs spilled healthily from numerous terracotta pots.

'Neither do I,' he said glancing at his feet then back at her, his eyes stormy.

'I thought you lived in an Old Town apartment,' she pushed, certain he'd mentioned that when he'd first applied for the position at the hospital. Why was he acting so weird?

He nodded. 'I used to, until recently.'

'Okay,' she said, still unsatisfied. Not that he owed her any explanation. Not that she was likely to get one either. 'You seem upset. Is the reason you haven't been at work because—' She glanced at the hallway and lowered her voice to harsh whisper, '—we slept together?'

His stare held hers. 'No. Who are you looking for? I live here alone.'

Lola placed a hand on her forehead, her own news shoved aside in the face of his cryptic responses. 'I just... I assumed...' She met his stare. 'I'm surprised, that's all. I didn't picture you living somewhere like this.'

'I inherited this house recently,' he said in explanation. 'From my father.' He spat the word with contempt and the pieces began to fall into place. 'I haven't yet decided if I'll be keeping it,' he went on, 'or torching the place instead.'

'Your father?' She stared, incredulous, her heart racing anew. 'You told me you never knew him.'

'I didn't.' His jaw clenched so she could practically hear his teeth grinding together. 'And fortunately, I never will. He died a month ago. This—' he spread his arms wide, '—is my legacy. The house, the estate, the title, the private beach down there...' He pointed to where the gardens sloped towards a picture perfect crescent-shaped bay. 'Not to mention the yacht, the cars and the very lucrative winemaking business that comes with it.' He pressed his lips together and scowled in disgust.

'Wow... That's quite the inheritance.' But why wouldn't he keep it? And why did he seem so... angry? 'Why would you torch such a stunning home?' She was procrastinating now. Finding any excuse to avoid telling him why she'd come. But she'd never seen him angry before. He was intimidating enough in his usual, neutral state. Would he be receptive to her life-changing news in his current frame of mind?

He stepped closer, passionately making his point. 'Because no manner of wealth, land or expensive toys can make up for thirty-five years of pretending that I didn't exist,' he said, a quiet kind of fury rolling off him like waves. 'He had all of this and more and yet never gave my mother a single euro to help raise me. Even though he knew of my existence.'

'I see,' she said quietly, her curiosity turning to dread and her stomach churning. 'I'm sorry.'

Her timing couldn't be any more appalling. He was clearly going through something momentous emotionally. How could she tell him about the baby now?

'Do you see?' he demanded, bracing his hands on the counter of the island. 'Because I can't get my head around it.'

She shrugged. 'Well...not really. I mean I understand how you must be feeling hurt, rejected, perhaps even grieving for someone you never had the opportunity to know, but—'

'I'll never grieve for that man,' he said, coldly. 'If I hadn't seen the paternity test results he had done on me when I was a child, with my own eyes, I'd deny that we could ever be related.'

'Why?' she asked frowning, nervous that his anger might extend to the paternity of *her* baby once she told him her news. 'Was he so bad? Wouldn't most people consider a legacy like this akin to a lottery win?'

He leaned closer, his stare burning into hers, like a jungle cat about to pounce. 'Do you know who once owned this house, the estate, the title? All of it?'

Lola shook her head, her stomach in knots. 'No, why should I? I'm a doctor. I don't move in these circles.' Not since she'd ended her engagement to Nicolás.

'Mauricio de la Rosa,' he said. 'King Octavio's uncle.'

She gasped, her hand covering her mouth. 'Are you serious? *He's* your father?'

He laughed bitterly. 'I'm afraid so. I'm the illegitimate son he always knew about but disowned and ignored.'

She reached out and touched his arm, her heart pounding with shock. His muscles tensed under her fingers as he gripped the edge of the counter once more. A wave of empathy washed over her and she wished she could hold him in her arms. But theirs wasn't that kind of a relationship.

'Xavier, I'm so sorry,' she said instead. Her heart ached for him. Both for the boy and the man who, she imagined, had always felt lost because he'd only known half his story.

Xavier tensed under her touch. His feelings too volatile to untangle in the face of the fierce intensity of his ongoing attraction to her, which should have faded but only seemed stronger. He had no idea why she'd come to his home when they'd agreed that their one night would be the extent of their relationship. When she was leaving Castilona soon. But desperate to be free of the turmoil of the past week—during which he'd discovered his true parentage, been slapped with this insult of an inheritance and had his entire world turned upside down—his body had responded to her the minute he'd seen her in his driveway. As if he were a drowning man in the ocean and she was the only life raft for miles.

'That must have been a terrible shock,' she said quietly. The scent of her fanned the craving he'd experienced daily since the night of the storm, when he'd discovered just how flammable their chemistry was. But unlike back then, when she'd looked at him with desire and wonder, as if he was something special, now he saw only pity in her eyes.

'What are you doing here, Lola?' he asked, changing the subject, the idea that she might treat him differently because he was the illegitimate son of the late regent who'd ruled for a time until his brother's son had come of age, adding to his frustration. Was this to be his life now? A title, land and an estate he didn't want? His actions compared to those of de la Rosa? His so-called father's reputation for ruthlessness would probably long outlive the man. But Xavier would fight, tooth and nail, every day for the rest of his life to be nothing like him.

'I...' She dropped her hand from his arm and blinked up at him, uncharacteristically hesitant where he'd never known her to be anything other than calm and confident.

'Lost for words?' he asked, tauntingly, shutting down his confusion and hurt, wishing he could once more lose himself inside her the way he had that night. But discipline was his ally. Just like he'd needed it every day for the past month in order to stay away from Lola Garcia and stick to their deal, he would employ it now that she was standing in his kitchen.

'Not at all.' She stood taller. 'I'm wondering what you plan to do?' she asked, swallowing as if her mouth was dry.

He glanced down at her soft red lips, desperate to hear them cry his name. Desperate for her to look at him with desire and infatuation. The way she had as he'd made her body sing, shoving her headlong into two orgasms that had utterly undone her polished, poised exterior.

'Will you resign as head of security at the clinic now that you have all this?' she asked, glancing around the luxurious space.

'Why would that be your concern?' he asked, sneering because he took pride in being judged by his actions, not his net worth. 'You're going back to Spain.'

Whereas Xavier was more confused about where he belonged than ever. Nothing about this inheritance felt right. He'd only moved into Casa Colina because the staff had questions about their jobs and needed reassurance that he wasn't certain he could give in the long term.

But having Lola this close, his entire body ached to crush her in his arms and to kiss her until she moaned and looked at him as if he was just a man she desperately wanted.

'Maybe I'll sell all this,' he said. 'Go back to my ordinary life.' He shrugged, his gaze clinging to her features. To the slope of her neck and the swell of her breasts. 'I don't need it. I'm just a simple guy after all.'

All he really wanted was to forget—his past, his renewed sense of rejection and betrayal and this stifling legacy he had no idea what to do with. Even Lola, who was after all moving on.

'Perhaps I'll donate the money to charity,' he went on. 'Change my name and move overseas so I can be anonymous again, because as soon as word spreads, there will be a lot more people looking at me with stunned contempt, as you're doing right now.'

Lola frowned and shook her head. 'I'm not looking at you that way. I'm shocked, yes, but all I feel for you is empathy. To not know your father all these years then to be left this...'

Xavier hadn't had a restful night's sleep since they'd slept together. Waking most nights from sweaty dreams, hard and aching for more of her passion. He reached out, cupped her jaw and tugged her bottom lip from under her teeth with the pad of his thumb. Tilting her eyes up to his so he saw a flicker of that passion she'd unleashed from her professional, put together demeanour that night.

'You still haven't told me why you're here,' he said, finding himself a step closer. 'Did you decide that one night wasn't enough? Or have you come to say goodbye?'

At the reminder he might never see her again,

desire roared through him, demanding he touch her until her moans of pleasure and the way she'd cried his name drowned out the fury and impotence in his head. He too was tempted to go back on their deal, if only to distract himself from the sharp turn his life had taken. Everything was crumbling. He'd always imagined that knowing who his father was would free him and slot his missing piece back into place. But if anything, he felt more unsettled. Adrift like those missing fishing boats taken by the storm. Who was he supposed to be with a title, land and a princess as a half-sister? With an estate to run and a historic aristocratic title to measure up to? It felt more like a cage than a lottery win.

'No,' she said, her stare clear and bold and full of her signature determination he found so compelling. She tilted her chin up. 'I came to tell you that I'm pregnant.'

Xavier's hand fell to his side. The breath whooshed out of him as if he'd been winded by a blow to the chest. 'What?'

'You heard me correctly,' she said, sounding instantly defensive. 'I'm pregnant and the baby is yours.'

Xavier reeled, his legs unsteady, his heart wrestling its way out of his chest as he gripped the edge of the counter. 'We used a condom,' he said, stunned, blurting out the first rational thing that came to his spinning mind.

'It happens,' she said with a shrug he was certain she didn't feel. 'I know. It's a shock.' Finally her voice turned sympathetic. 'I only took a test this morning, so I'm still reeling, too. But I wanted to tell you as soon as possible. Obviously, I knew nothing about what you've been going through here, otherwise I might have left it for another time.'

Confused, Xavier latched onto her words in an attempt to claw back some control of his life.

'What does that mean?' he asked, adding dread to the other emotions spinning inside him like a whirlwind. 'You're supposed to be leaving Castilona for Spain soon. When else would you have told me?'

Would she have left the country with his baby? Maybe even raised it alone and kept it from him? His stomach churned. It was as if history was repeating. As if she might leave and force Xavier into the absentee parent role his sperm donor had chosen. Force Xavier to be like the man he felt no connection to whatsoever. Well he might be stunned by her news, but one thing was for certain—*his* child would know exactly who its father was.

'I don't know,' she snapped. 'I'm here telling you now, aren't I? But don't worry. As far as I'm concerned, nothing's changed. I don't want anything from you.' She raised her chin. 'I don't need anything either. I work hard so I can support myself and the baby. And you're right, I'll be going home to Spain soon, so I'll have my family to help out.'

Xavier stiffened, not sure he was hearing her correctly. 'Hold on a second...' He held up his hand, the room all but tilting. 'You're *still* leaving Castilona?'

This week just kept getting better and better... She'd not only dropped this bombshell when he was trying to come to terms with the fact his entire life had been a shameful secret, but she'd also decided she didn't need his help and was taking his baby away.

She flushed. 'Of course. As soon as I finish working my notice. I've applied to work for a medical relief organisation, although they probably won't want me now...so I'll have to think of something else. I might go back to university.'

He stepped closer, narrowing his eyes, taking no satisfaction from the way her pupils dilated as she looked up at him. 'So this was just a courtesy call before you leave the country with our baby? What if I want to be a part of my child's life? Where do I fit into the equation, Lola?'

She frowned, blinking. 'I assumed—'

'You assumed that because I never knew *my* own father, I would want nothing to do with my son or daughter?' Fury left him deadly still. 'How very presumptuous of you.'

'No...of course not.' Her frown deepened and

her cheeks coloured. 'I didn't mean that. It's just that we're not a couple, so I assumed this would be complicated... That we'd need to come to some sort of custody arrangement.'

'We will.' Xavier nodded. His resolve strengthened because in a split second the world he'd felt was crumbling had settled, its pieces sliding back into place. He was going to be a father. Something he'd never really considered because he'd always shied away from serious relationships. But now that it was happening, there was no way he'd inflict the same fate he'd experienced on his own child.

'How are we to come to any sort of arrangement if you're in Spain?' he asked. 'Or worse, performing medical procedures in a tent in some war-torn country, which is dangerous and frankly ridiculous?'

Her stare narrowed, determination flattening her mouth. 'It's possible. Women can do more than one thing in this day and age you know,' she said sarcastically. Then she swallowed, looking contrite. 'But you're right. I haven't figured everything out yet.'

'I guess I should be grateful for the fact you didn't simply keep this to yourself, leave Castilona and never tell me about my child. Never tell our child who its father is.'

When he'd confided in her that night of the

storm, he'd never imagined it would be used against him this way.

She gasped, horrified. 'I would never do that. That's abhorrent. I can't believe you're even suggesting it.'

'You'll forgive me,' he said bitterly. 'My experience with fathers is limited, as you know.'

She winced then and moved closer. 'Look... Why don't we talk again in a few days when we've both had a chance to come to terms with this news. We both have a lot going on at the moment. I don't know...maybe you can visit me in Spain and we can...come up with a plan.'

'A plan?' he asked, incredulous, the idea of him having no contact or say in the life of the baby they'd made together making him panic. 'You can't take my child out of the country, just like that,' he said, still stung by the fact that his own mother had kept his paternity from him although her motivation had been to keep him safe. The de la Rosas were a powerful family and Mauricio had been the most ruthless of them all. As a cook in the palace kitchens, Carlota Torres had been at a distinct disadvantage, both emotionally and financially.

'Well I can't leave it with you either, can I?' she snapped, placing one hand on her hip. 'And don't forget, I'm my own person too.'

They faced each other angrily. All the pent-up frustration he felt at his change of circumstances boiled over, directed at Lola. 'You can delay your departure, until we sort things out,' he said, his mind racing.

She shook her head adamant. 'I dislike being told what I can and cannot do. And besides, I've ended my tenancy on my rented house. I have to leave. I have nowhere else to live.'

'I'm not telling,' he said, moderating his tone of voice. 'I'm suggesting.'

But now that the initial shock had worn off, the full implications of this came at him, thick and fast. If she left with his baby, he might never see either of them again. Not to mention that now he'd inherited all this, he'd begun to attract media attention. There were paparazzi camped on his street as they spoke. He knew how intrusive they could be from his years of keeping Princess Xiomara safe. There was no way a child of his would be exposed to that. If nothing else, he would keep his baby safe.

'Do you realise...' he started to ask, his voice calm while panic slithered through his veins, '...that if the Castilonian laws of secession change, as is currently being debated by parliament, this baby, *our* baby, will effectively be fourth in line to the throne after the twin princes and Princess Xiomara?'

She paled, her eyes wide. 'No...' she whispered.

Xavier nodded. 'It's time for a reality check, Lola. Even if our child is never recognised as legitimate because Mauricio de la Rosa was a scoundrel who knocked up the palace cook and then persuaded her it was in my best interests to never know my parentage, our child will still have royal blood. Still have all of this one day.' He stretched out his arms, now certain exactly what he would do with the unwanted legacy he'd inherited. 'Whether we like it or not, that will make our child a target and safety is my job.'

'Don't say that,' she said, shaking her head in disbelief. 'That's not true.'

'I assume you saw the paps outside?' Xavier pinned her with his stare. 'They've been there all week since news of Mauricio's death. Our baby will move in ruthless circles that are all about power and wealth. He or she will need protection from stalkers, kidnappers, the press. I, for one, will do anything to ensure their safety.'

'But I'm just an ordinary woman,' she cried. 'A doctor. You can't hold me captive simply because *you've* inherited a legacy that two minutes ago you didn't even want.'

There was less fight in her voice and more fear. He wished he hadn't needed to put the latter there, but she needed to understand the consequences of their one night together, which transcended both of them.

'I'm not imprisoning you Lola,' he said quietly, stepping back to appear less threatening. 'But you should know this—I will be a father to our child. Every day for the rest of my life.'

'Of course,' she said. 'I'd never stop you from seeing the baby.'

He nodded, nowhere near appeased. 'I'm glad to hear that. Because my second job, after being a father, will be to keep our child safe,' he went on as if she hadn't interrupted. 'Even if I have to fight you to do it. I'd prefer that we worked together, but it's your choice.'

'But… I…' She clenched her fists in frustration and searched his stare.

Xavier held his ground, still processing the news he'd never have imagined when he awoke that morning.

'Oh… I can't talk to you right now,' she said petulantly. 'Not when you're being so…unreasonable. I'll be in touch in a few days.'

And with that, she stormed out.

CHAPTER SEVEN

As the outgoing clinical director of the *Clinico San Carlos*, Lola had been invited to the annual Royal Garden Party at the palace a week later—an event coveted by every member of the Castilonian elite. Not that she was in the mood for a party, but it wouldn't do to decline highly influential benefactors like King Octavio and Queen Phoebe.

Seeking solace from the crowds, Lola traipsed through the stunning rose gardens at the palace, her bare shoulders warmed by the spring sunshine, which was putting on its best display for the event. Taking a sip of her perfectly chilled and refreshing virgin mimosa, Lola marvelled at the sheer number of heavily scented varieties in bloom. But her mind wasn't distracted for long. She was still confused by her last conversation with Xavier and was still childishly ignoring his calls.

She tried to see things from his point of view, but how dare he tell her what to do. She understood how his inheritance must have come as a massive shock, but she was a modern woman with a career. Not an aristocratic brood mare, happy to pump out children to keep some ancient family line going.

At that mean-spirited thought, hot shame washed over her. Xavier wasn't Nicolás. He didn't want a wife. And he must be feeling so conflicted about his inheritance given his father's former years of rejection. Of course he would want to be a better father that that, which wouldn't be hard... She guessed she should be happy that he wanted to be involved with their baby, but it was so...complicated.

'Ignoring my calls won't change the facts,' a voice said. *His* voice.

She spun, startled, her reply dying on her tongue as she took him in. Apart from that one time at his home, when he'd been wearing worn jeans and t-shirt, she'd never seen him out of his security uniform of black trousers and polo shirt. Now, dressed in taupe chinos, a blue dress shirt open at the collar and an olive green linen sports jacket, he looked utterly delicious. Every inch a member of the European aristocracy.

'I needed some space,' she said, trying to shut down her body's instantaneous reaction——her blood overheating, her breathing tight, her pulse surging. 'We gave each other quite a lot to think about that day. And as it stands right now, I'm not sure I have anything new to say to you,' she said, noticing how he'd had his hair cut a little shorter at the collar, making it seem a little longer on top. His facial hair was neatly trimmed. The perfect amount of sexy scruff to make her want to kiss him, just to feel the scrape of it against her skin, because as much as she disliked his heavy handedness, their chemistry was as inarguable as ever. And never more irrelevant.

'In that case, I hope you managed to clear your head,' he said, watching her from behind his dark sunglasses.

How dare he look so handsome and composed when she was so instantly flustered.

'What are you doing here?' she asked changing the subject. 'Not at the garden party, but here in the rose garden. Shouldn't you be over there making small talk?' She assumed his recent status change had prompted his invitation to the party unless he was there as a former member of staff.

Xavier slung his hands casually into his trouser pockets and glanced to where most people were gathered on the immaculate lawns, enjoying chilled champagne and gourmet canapés delivered by formally attired wait staff.

'I...um...seem to have reached my capacity for small talk,' he said. 'As a newcomer to both elite society and wine growing, what I can offer to the conversation is limited anyway. I have no idea which socialite is marrying which billionaire this summer or how fruitful the grape harvest is likely to be this year.'

Taking pity on him, because he was clearly out of his comfort zone despite appearing as if he belonged, Lola stepped closer, smiling slightly. 'It's easy,' she said, lowering her voice. 'In my experience, people with power, wealth and influence like to talk about themselves. All you have to do is ask them what they do for a living and they'll fill in any conversational blanks. Then it's simply a case of nodding occasionally.'

Neither of them truly belonged here, among the famous and influential and royal, although Lola had yet to see the King and Queen who were purported to be joining the party at some point.

'Thanks for the tip.' Rare amusement twitched his lips.

She wished he'd remove the sunglasses so she could see his eyes.

'But I'd much rather talk to you,' he said quietly. 'How are you feeling?' His gaze dipped to her stomach as if she was already showing, which of course she wasn't. But with the exception of Isla, the baby was their little secret.

'I'm okay,' she said with a small sigh, unable to stay angry with him now that he'd lost the bossy tone of the previous week. 'Sore boobs, going to the toilet all the time and this morning I felt decidedly nauseous. Apart from that, I'm awesome,' she finished sarcastically.

She left out the hormonal mood swings that left her wanting to throttle him one minute and have sex with him the next. Sadly neither was an option.

'Is there anything I can do to help?' he asked, his lips pursed in a small frown, his concern for her wellbeing obviously genuine.

'I think you've done enough, don't you?' She laughed softly.

He didn't laugh along, merely clenched his jaw and glanced at the ground. 'I… I want to be there for you both, which is probably what I should have said last week. I might have come over a little harsh the last time we spoke. So…apologies.'

'A little?' she teased because she could see that he was trying and neither of them had planned this.

'There was a lot coming at me,' he said, serious, his voice turned gruff with repressed emotion. 'But I meant what I said—I want to help raise our child. I want to…protect you both. I hope we can talk and find a way for us to figure this out together.'

Lola shuddered, his protectiveness awakening some primitive desire in her that she would have previously denied. Common sense told her he'd included her in his statement because for the next eight months, wherever she went, their baby went too. But no matter how hard she tried, because she was a strong, independent woman, she couldn't forget the way she'd felt wrapped in those strong arms of his—safe, seen, respected. The way he'd groaned her name in that gravelly voice as he'd climaxed. The way he then turned tender, holding her face in his palms and staring into her eyes as if they'd just shared something special. Which, as it had turned out, they had. They'd made their child that night.

'Of course, Xavier,' she said, her voice breaking. 'I want that too.'

They stared at each other in silence. A kind of truce forming. But then just as they seemed to be entering new conciliatory territory, there was a crunch of gravel behind them.

'Dr Garcia,' a breathless uniformed staff member interrupted. 'There's a medical emergency with one of the guests. Are you able to come to the drawing room right away?'

'Of course,' Lola said, thrusting her glass of juice at the young woman.

'I'll come too,' Xavier said and they hurried after a second staff member who showed them the way.

They ran through a series of exquisite rooms and marble tiled hallways, finally entering a vast elegant drawing room with a large marble fireplace, art bedecked walls and French doors framed by billowing white drapes that opened onto a terrace.

The patient, a man in his sixties, was seated on

the edge of a cream upholstered sofa. A similarly aged woman fretted at his side.

'I'm Dr Garcia,' Lola said, reaching for the man's wrist and taking his pulse, which was fast but regular. 'Can you tell me what happened?'

'Pain...' the man said, clearly breathless and sweating, his complexion alarmingly grey.

'He has a pain in his chest,' the woman supplied. 'His name is Lorenzo and I'm Carmen, his wife.'

'Does your husband have any medical history?' Lola asked, aware that Xavier stood just behind. She noted that Lorenzo was overweight. His rotund belly stretching at his shirt buttons.

'Just arthritis,' she replied, concerned.

Lola turned to the steward in the room. 'Has an ambulance been called?' The party continued outside, but the last thing they needed was for a full-blown medical incident at the palace.

'Yes, Dr Garcia,' the man said.

'Do you have any aspirin at the palace?' she asked as Xavier helped Lorenzo loosen his tie and the top button of his shirt.

'We've sent for the palace's first aid box, ma'am,' the steward replied. 'Ah, here it is now.' He took the large box from another man and placed it on the table beside them.

Lola opened the box, finding a fully equipped medical kit, including a blood pressure machine, a stethoscope and even an automated external defibrillator, or AED.

'Aspirin,' Xavier said, holding up the bottle. His stare on hers was calm and reassuring, as it had been the night of the storm, filling her with confidence that no matter what was thrown their way, they could handle it together.

'Can we have a glass of water?' Xavier asked the steward, who nodded and retrieved one from a sideboard at the end of the room.

Lola fitted the stethoscope in her ears and, with Xavier's help, raised the man's shirt so she could listen to his chest at the back.

While the patient swallowed the aspirin, and with her examination complete, she drew Xavier aside. 'I think he's having a myocardial infarction,' she whispered, glancing nervously at the door. 'I'd feel happier if the ambulance and paramedics were here.'

Xavier wrapped his hand around her elbow, his touch warm and comforting. 'You stay with Lorenzo. I'll speak to the steward and ensure that we can admit the ambulance to the palace grounds with the minimum of delay. The guests and press outside are a logistical problem, but there's a rear way out. We can transport him to the ambulance that way, avoiding a scene.'

Lola nodded, her hand covering his before she was even aware that she'd moved. 'Thank you.' She held his stare for a few seconds, yet again grateful that he was there to help. Even if she'd been free to speak in that moment, she doubted she'd find the words.

While Xavier discreetly discussed logistics with the palace staff, Lola returned to the patient. 'I'm concerned that you might be having a heart attack, Lorenzo,' she explained to the man and his wife. 'The aspirin should help before the ambulance arrives, but what we really need is for you to be assessed at hospital where they can run blood tests and look more closely at your heart.'

'Should I drive him there?' Carmen asked, clutching the pearls at her throat.

Lola shook her head, but before she could add that waiting for the ambulance was safest, Lorenzo slumped to the side and rolled onto the floor, unconscious.

'Xavier,' Lola called.

Xavier bounded over and knelt opposite her while they each felt for a pulse.

'Help me roll him over,' she said, struggling with the patient who had turned into a dead weight and was too heavy for her alone.

With the patient lying on his back, she felt again for a carotid pulse, her suspicions turning to dread when she failed to find one. 'No pulse,' she told Xavier, their eyes meeting for a split second.

Xavier looked up from listening for breath sounds. 'No breathing either.'

'He's in cardiac arrest,' Lola said to the steward while Xavier delivered two rescue breaths via mouth to mouth. 'Have someone re-call emergency services to let them know and unpack the defibrillator,' she instructed, while commencing chest compressions.

At the count of thirty, she paused for Xavier to administer another two rescue breaths, a horrible sense of déjà vu coming over her. Last time they'd been in this position, the night of the storm, they'd lost the patient. Lola couldn't bear the idea of that happening again, here at the palace with the man's wife watching on as she sobbed into a lace trimmed handkerchief.

Beginning another cycle of chest compressions, Lola glanced at Xavier, whose expression was calmly neutral. But because she knew him better, she saw he was thinking the same thing. By the time of her next pause, the steward had switched on the defibrillator and Xavier had stuck the electrodes onto the man's chest. Lola observed the heart's rhythm displayed on the machine's small screen.

'He's in VF,' she told Xavier who nodded, delivering two final breaths.

When the machine instructed them to stand clear, they removed their hands from the patient to allow the two-hundred-volt shock to be given.

To Lola's relief, the heart returned to sinus rhythm. 'There's a pulse,' she said as Lorenzo groaned, still groggy and semi-conscious, as he tried to bat them away.

'The paramedics have arrived,' the steward said in a panicked voice, moving to a door on the other side of the room and swinging it open to admit the ambulance crew.

As the paramedics placed an oxygen mask over Lorenzo's face and transferred him to a stretcher, Lola gave them a brief history of events. Within minutes, they'd whisked both the patient and his tearful wife from the room, leaving Lola, Xavier and the steward alone.

'Thank you, Dr Garcia,' the steward said, clearing away the equipment they'd used so the elegant, sun-bathed drawing room was once more immaculate, showing no sign of what had transpired there. 'Do take your time. You won't be disturbed here.'

He discreetly left and closed the door.

Drained of adrenaline and unusually emotional, Lola shivered, goosebumps erupting over her bare arms. From behind, Xavier silently draped his soft linen sports coat over her shoulders, the fabric giving off the warmth from his body and the scent of his after shave.

'Come on,' he said, his arm around her shoulders. 'I'll drive you home. One of my old security guard buddies can deliver your car later.'

'Thanks,' she said, meekly following him from the room to the parking area at the rear of the palace, away from where the garden party continued unsuspecting.

'I don't know what's wrong with me...' she said as she clicked her seatbelt into place.

'It's just shock,' he said, reaching for her hand and squeezing. 'You came here expecting to socialise in the sun, not to resuscitate someone in the palace drawing room.'

She nodded, grateful once more for his calm, reassuring presence.

'We're making a habit of tackling medical emergencies together,' he said as they headed down the palace's rear driveway, hoping to make her smile because she'd fallen pale and quiet.

Grateful for his inherited car's tinted windows, Xavier paused at the electronic gates before he drove past the handful of paps loitering outside the palace hoping to photograph a member of the royal family or someone rich and famous leaving the party, and headed for the city.

She glanced over at him, a ghost of a smile on her lovely lips. 'I agree. We really have to stop meeting like that.' She sighed tiredly and frustration coiled tight inside him.

He fought the instinct to touch her again. Things were complicated enough between them without indulging the pretty constant need to kiss her to see if it was as good as he remembered.

Not that he needed the test to be certain of the outcome.

'Apart from the unforeseen cardiac arrest...' she said, glancing his way with a little more colour in her cheeks, '...how was your first official social event as *Marqués de Moro*? I saw the story announcing the death of Mauricio on the news.'

Xavier paused at traffic lights, shooting her a mocking look. 'If I admit that I hated every second until I found you in the rose garden, would you be shocked?' he asked, his pulse accelerating because she looked lovely, her slim figure draped in a floaty summer dress.

He'd done his best to hide from the breaking news, from the paps eager to get a shot of the shocking illegitimate heir no one knew about, but they'd still somehow found him, snapping pictures outside the hospital as he'd arrived for his shift.

'It's surely not that bad.' Lola watched him for a few seconds, until he looked away and pulled off once more.

'I don't belong,' he said with a shrug. 'And what's more, I don't care. But everyone else knows I'm a fish out of water and they *do* seem to care. For the moment at least, until I become old news.'

'I understand how you feel you know,' she said quietly. 'Maybe better than you think.'

When he shot her a quizzical look, she went

on. 'I told you I was engaged,' she said pensively. 'If I'd gone through with it, I'd have married into that kind of family—obscenely wealthy, influential, titled. Nicolás and I were young when we met, but then after we got engaged, his expectations changed. I began to see that as far as he and his family were concerned, my dreams, my ambitions, were irrelevant. He talked about us running the estate together. About raising our family to take over one day. And when I insisted that I still wanted to go to medical school and become a doctor, he laughed.'

'Why would he laugh?' Xavier scowled, annoyed on Lola's behalf.

'He said that as his wife, I wouldn't need to work. He completely missed the point that I wanted to do something I could be proud of. Something for myself. When I kept pushing for his agreement that I could follow my own dreams, he gave me an ultimatum.'

Xavier held his breath, knowing strong, spirited Lola would have hated that.

'He said if I loved him, I'd work with him. When I pointed out that it worked both ways, that if he loved me and the person I am he'd want me to do whatever made me happy, he refused to see it.'

'So you called things off?'

She nodded. 'I went to medical school, became

a doctor and embarked on a fulfilling career. I'm proud of what I've achieved.'

'Do you have any regrets about...the relationship?' he asked, keeping his eyes on the road. She didn't belong to him, but because she was having his baby, because he couldn't wipe that night from his mind, he couldn't ignore the panic that came whenever he thought of her leaving Castilona. The idea of her past feelings for this other man burned his chest with hot stabs of jealousy.

'No,' she said. 'I always imagined having a loving relationship like the one my parents have. My mother's family wanted her to marry someone professional, but she fell in love with my dad, an artist, and married him anyway. Nicolás obviously didn't love *me*. And I thought I loved him but realised I hadn't known the real him at all. I wanted more than to fill my days with charity work and running his ancient estate in which I had no interest. Of course the irony of the fact that, before I knew I was pregnant, I'd resigned from my job to work for an overseas charity isn't lost on me.' She huffed softly, her eyes falling to her lap. 'So you see, I understand how you feel about your inheritance. How on the surface it can seem like a gift, but if it's not who you truly are it becomes more like a cage.'

Xavier nodded, her heartfelt admissions leaving him unsettled. But she was right. She could understand that what appeared from the outside as a very generous and life-changing gift could, from the inside, feel claustrophobic.

'If it wasn't for the baby,' he said quietly, 'I seriously would have donated the entire estate to charity.'

'You still could...' she said, her hand resting over her belly.

He nodded grimly, because in some ways, he had no choice but to accept the legacy. 'I don't plan on disowning my child. Do you think once the media, those paps back at the palace, learn of our child's existence that we'll be able to walk away from its birthright? That title has been handed down from father to son since the sixteenth century. I have a theory that that's why de la Rosa passed it on to me. He had no legitimate son and, as power hungry as he was, his ego finally outweighed his need to reject me as his.'

She touched his arm. 'It may not be that simple...'

'Even if I refuse the inheritance,' he went on, ignoring the misplaced credit she attributed to de la Rosa, 'the estate and title will be kept in trust for our child. And besides, since I've moved in to Casa Colina and seen how the estate is run for myself, I've had to think twice about throwing it all away. There are many families whose livelihoods are tied to the estate. They are reliant on the income to feed their children and pay their mortgages. It's no longer just about me and my wants.'

'I see,' Lola said. 'But then life is never straightforward, is it?'

They drove in silence for a few minutes, through the busy streets of the capital. Xavier pulled up outside her apartment and turned off the engine.

'I'll walk you in,' he said, jumping from the car and opening her door.

'Thanks.' She took her key from her purse. They entered the building and climbed the stairs to the first floor.

Inside her apartment, the entire place was stacked with packing boxes, a sickening reminder that she was moving on. Lola removed Xavier's jacket and, shivering again, reached for a hoodie from a pile of folded clothes on the sofa before slipping it on.

'I hope you've employed a moving company,' he said gruffly, those protective urges returning. She was so independent and he had all these... urges. He wanted to make her tea, run her a bath and carry all her possessions for her. What the hell was happening to him?

'I will,' she said, collecting his jacket and holding it out to him.

He took it, their fingers brushing for a second, before they each pulled away. But that second of contact was enough to all but choke him with a surge of desire. How could he still want her so badly when they'd agreed to move on? When everything was complicated now, because she was having his baby? When nothing was settled and she might soon be leaving the country?

'I guess I'll need to find somewhere else to rent,' she said, 'until…you know, we sort everything out. Not that I'm sure what I'll be doing next…'

'Aside from becoming a mother.' Xavier stepped closer, as if his feet weren't under his control.

'Yes.' She smiled. 'Aside from that.'

'You could stay with me,' he said, stunning himself. 'That house has twenty-two bedrooms and a separate, self-contained guest house. It's so big we wouldn't even run into each other.'

If she moved in, he could help her out and be involved. Of course, there'd be pros and cons to having her under the same roof. He could protect her and gain the peace of mind that would come with knowing she and the baby were safe. But, conversely, the physical proximity might become a form of torture. His restraint would only stretch so far.

'I don't think that's a good idea,' she said, as if she could read his mind.

He nodded. 'I agree… It was just a suggestion.'

She shot him a look of surprise.

'But we could avoid each other if we had to.' His stare dipped to her lips, which were parted, her breathing fast and shallow. 'I've been trying to avoid you since I came to work at the hospital so I'm well practised.' His admission made his pulse buzz in his fingertips, but the time for pretence had been and gone. They'd proved how badly they'd wanted each other. They'd even made a baby.

'Why?' she whispered, a small frown tugging at her mouth.

Xavier paused, not sure she'd like his answer. 'What happened between us the night of the storm,' he said, 'I'd wanted you since we first met.'

Her breathing sped up, her lips parted. 'And that's a bad thing?' she asked, looking confused and so beautiful, he couldn't breathe.

He shrugged, wishing she would step away, because he seemed to lack the strength. 'I told you. I only do casual. I assumed you were a for ever kind of woman, not to mention you were my boss.'

Xavier imagined he saw a flicker of something like disappointment pass over her face. 'I guess I am a for ever kind of woman, with the right man.'

Xavier nodded, that jealous twist of his gut returning. 'I knew it,' he said, trying for humour. But he didn't feel like laughing.

Of course *he* could never be the right man. He'd never been in love. Not even close. Love was all about belonging. Something he knew nothing about. He'd just about come to terms with who he was and then bam, the letter from de la Rosa's solicitor had arrived. And now he was going to be a father, another thing of which he had no experience. What if he turned out to be like his father? No, he would never allow that to happen.

'I'm sorry I ignored your calls,' she said quietly.

'It's okay.'

'I guess I've always known where I was headed and now... I'm all over the place,' she said.

He nodded, compassion squeezing his lungs. 'We're both going through some changes.'

'Yes.' She looked uncertain. He'd never seen her that way.

If he didn't leave soon he might touch her, hold her and struggle to stop there.

'Have something to eat,' he said instead, stepping back at last. He draped the jacket over his arm and shoved his hands into his pockets. 'Drink tea maybe. You still look...pale.'

She inhaled, as if she was about to say something more, then appeared to change her mind. 'I...will.'

At the door, he paused, turning to face her once more. 'When you're next free, I'd appreciate a chance to talk about the baby. There are plans we need to make.' He would start as he meant to go on with fatherhood, be fully involved from the beginning, letting his child know exactly how much he or she was loved and wanted.

'Okay.' She followed him to the threshold. 'Thanks for your help earlier and for the lift.'

'Get some rest,' he said, fighting the urge to press a kiss to her cheek, because they weren't friends and he couldn't trust that he'd be able to resist.

Instead, he walked away, tossed his jacket on the passenger seat and drove home, the scent of her perfume she'd left behind taunting him every mile of the journey.

CHAPTER EIGHT

The following Monday, after a weekend spent pointlessly reliving every second of her final frustrating conversation with Xavier, Lola was at her desk when she received a summons to the hospital's security office.

Embarrassed by the eager clack of her heels against the marble tiles as she hurried there assuming the call had come from Xavier, she paused outside the room to pull herself together and steady her excited breaths.

'Dr Garcia,' Antonio, one of the regular security guards, said standing as she entered the small room, which was equipped with a wall of screens capturing images from the multiple cameras around the hospital.

'You wanted to see me,' Lola said with smile, hiding her disappointment that Xavier was absent.

'Yes, ma'am. We have a situation.'

With a couple of mouse clicks, Antonio brought up an enlarged image, the live feed of the camera that faced the hospital's main entrance. Across the street stood a cluster of paps, smoking, chatting and raising their cameras to their faces every time a car slowed as if it might pull into the clinic's private driveway.

'They've been there since five a.m.,' Antonio said.

'Who do they want?' she asked, peering closer, her stomach flopping with dread. It could only be Xavier. There was no one else particularly newsworthy currently on the premises.

'I don't know, ma'am. Shall I call the police?' Antonio asked.

Lola straightened, frustration whipping through her. 'No. They're on a public footpath. They're not breaking any laws. Let's just hope they soon get bored or hungry or dash off to bother someone else.'

Just as she was leaving the security office, she came face to face with Xavier. Unlike at the garden party the weekend before, he was now clean shaven, but just as devastatingly handsome.

'Dr Garcia,' he said, his stare shifting over her face and briefly lower to the V-neck of her blouse, reminding her of the way he'd looked at her when he'd dropped her home the other night—as if he was struggling to walk away. But maybe he simply wanted to discuss the baby again.

'I hope you had a restful weekend,' he said, as if oblivious to the havoc he'd caused with his casual comment about wanting her since they'd first met. It shouldn't have made any difference, but she hadn't been able to stop thinking about him all weekend.

'Thank you. I did,' she said, her stomach swooping at his proximity. 'Would you walk with me, please?'

She headed back towards her office with Xavier at her side. 'Have you seen our friends across the street?'

He nodded, his mouth pressed into a line. 'I have, I'm afraid. I think this time, they're after me. They've also been camped opposite my gates since I moved into Casa Colina.' He paused at the threshold to her office and faced her. 'Which is why you'll find my letter of resignation in your email inbox.'

Shocked, Lola stepped inside her office, gesturing him to follow. 'You're leaving us?' she asked ridiculously given that she too was leaving *Clinico San Carlos*. 'Are you sure?'

The paps would soon lose interest. Hopefully…

He stood just inside the door. 'Yes, ma'am.'

'Do you have another job lined up?' It wasn't what she wanted to ask. She wished he'd closed the door so they could have a personal conversation, but she was desperately trying to stay professional. Trying to keep her distance as effortlessly as he was able, even though sometimes, she wanted to hurl herself into his arms and kiss him.

'No,' he said, his stare holding hers. 'I'm going

to be concentrating on some personal matters for the time being.'

They stared at each other, some kind of weird telepathic communication connecting them. Was he saying he'd decided to embrace his inheritance? Or was he talking about fatherhood? Either option left her itchy, as if his choices had consequences for her independence, which she guessed they did in a way. He would likely have the same reservations about her leaving Castilona, which, if she imagined the tables were turned, wasn't that unreasonable. She wouldn't tolerate him taking their child overseas without her, either.

Lola swallowed her throat dry as doubts filled her head. 'Then I wish you well, Xavier,' she said, her voice thankfully steady. 'I'll happily provide a reference, should you ever need it in future.'

'Thank you.'

He was doing that military stance thing again. His hands clasped behind his back as they stared at each other. She wanted to rattle him as he effortlessly flustered her with his reasonable requests, honest admissions and potent virility.

Before she could inappropriately raise their personal issues, he stepped closer, his stiff posture softening. 'Have dinner with me tonight,' he said quietly. 'So we can talk.'

Lola's heart galloped with excitement, even as the urge to point out that he was telling her what to do again built on her tongue. But he was too close, smelled too good, the look in his eyes both vulnerable and expectant. She couldn't disappoint him.

'What time?' she asked, enslaved suddenly by the crackle of sexual tension that had always existed between them and had in no way diminished since they'd slept together.

'Why don't we leave here together tonight, sneak past the paps. My car has tinted windows.'

'Okay,' she said, a thrill of anticipation fluttering in her stomach. But it was just a meal and a conversation. If only her hormone-ridden body understood that.

'If that's all then…?' he asked, effortlessly resuming his professional role where Lola was left achy and breathless, her body pityingly desperate for their physical connection. She needed to be careful. Surrendering to lust was one thing but losing her head over a man who was always in control of his emotions…that would be a very stupid mistake.

Later that evening, Xavier carefully poured Lola a glass of iced lemonade made by his housekeeper, Tia. The cavernous kitchen somehow felt warmer and more inviting now that Lola was there to share it. Their journey from the clinic to Casa Colina had of course attracted interest from the photographers camped across the street. His car was recognisable and several paps had followed them on mopeds. But thanks to the clinic's underground car park, as well as Casa Colina's electric gates and long drive, they'd been able to get a head start and hopefully avoided providing any profitable photos. That hadn't eased Xavier's concern though. He knew firsthand how...persistent some of them could be.

'I wondered who you might have told,' he said, sliding the lemonade across the counter. 'About the baby?'

He returned to the hob, lowered the burner under the vegetable paella and gave it one final stir.

'I've told my twin sister, Isla. That's all,' she said, watching him cook with a slightly impressed expression he enjoyed.

'If it's okay with you...' he said, '... I'd like to tell my mother. I think she's pretty much given up hope that I would meet someone I'd be serious about, so she's going to be thrilled to be an *abuela* at last. She will, of course, be discreet. Working at the palace she's had plenty of practice. And I'll make sure to explain that we're not together.'

'Of course,' Lola said, glancing over her shoulder. 'Is she here? Will she be moving in?'

'No. She's still coming to terms with all of this,' he said, trying and failing to keep the bitterness from his voice. 'De la Rosa seduced her when she was young and vulnerable then got angry when she told him she was pregnant. He convinced her to keep his secret, said it was for my own protection, but no one benefited from that more than him.'

'Her hesitation is understandable,' she said. 'Have you considered how he might have done you a favour, even if it was for his own ends?'

'By leaving me a tainted legacy you mean?'

'No. More like his selfishness gave you a chance to grow up in private and follow your own dreams. I imagine having those paps follow you everywhere is pretty tedious. Just imagine if you'd had to cast aside your dreams of the army to come and work here, making wine because that was expected of you and not a choice.'

'I hadn't thought of it that way,' he said. 'And you're right about the paps. Nothing sells like a scandal. I think they'll lose interest in me soon though. Would you like a tour of the house?' he asked, removing the paella from the heat. 'Given that all of this will belong to our baby one day.'

With every day that passed, Xavier grew more and more comfortable in the role of caretaker. That he could someday turn an unwanted legacy from a man he'd never known into a safe and secure future for their child, helped him to rationalise it all.

'Sure,' she said, sliding from the stool.

Before they'd left the hospital, she'd changed into a long sun dress that might have been designed specifically to torture him given the way it caressed her figure, outlining her perfect breasts and trim waist, the flare of her hips and sexy backside. And she smelled like a meadow of flowers baked by the sun.

Trying to keep his distance, Xavier led her from the kitchen through the terracotta tiled hall to a whitewashed living room with French doors that overlooked the terraces of the garden.

'I hired some decorators to freshen up the place. It was a little dated,' he told her as they walked along.

'There's a library through there,' he said pointing down another corridor off the living room. 'A home office, gym and indoor pool too.'

'It's stunning,' she said, glancing around impressed, taking in the luxurious furnishings and original art on the walls.

Taking the stairs, he moved the tour to the first floor. 'There are four bedrooms at this end of the house. Eighteen more throughout the guest wing. Although who would ever need that many guests is beyond me,' he muttered, embarrassed by the extravagance he couldn't quite believe was his. Xavier was a simple man with simple needs.

'Might be useful for parties,' she suggested, laughing at him when he glanced her way in horror.

Then she poked her head into the first two bedrooms, her eyes wide. 'Very nice.'

'This staircase brings you to the back of the

house,' he said leading the way. 'There are quarters for the housekeeper,' he said, breezing past Tia's rooms. 'And here,' he swung open the door to a tiled courtyard and the separate, self-contained chalet beyond, 'is the guest house. Just in case you have even more guests, I guess.'

She shot him a sympathetic smile. 'It's impressive,' she said quietly as if mindful of his turbulent feelings.

'It's unnecessary,' he replied, sighing. 'Would you like to eat out here? The courtyard is sheltered from the breeze.'

'That would be lovely,' she said.

'Take a seat and I'll be back in a second.'

Xavier loaded up a tray with two plates of paella, the lemonade and glasses, cutlery and napkins. When he returned, Lola was staring out at the ocean, watching the sunset.

'So what do you plan to do now that you'll no longer be working security at the hospital?' she asked when he'd taken the seat next to hers.

'The estate supports sixty staff.' Xavier loaded up his fork with paella. 'As much as I'd love to board the place up and sleep in a hammock in the garden, I don't want to create any unemployment. There are staff here who've worked for the estate manager for close to twenty years.'

Lola nodded. 'That makes sense. So you're going to become a winemaker?'

Xavier scoffed softly. 'I might need to get some

qualifications to do that. I'm told it's a cross between an art form and a science, neither of which I know the first thing about.' He topped up her lemonade. 'In the short term, I'll spend some time here, learn how things work and figure out where I can be most useful. It might be by staying out of the way.'

'I'm glad,' she said, watching him carefully. 'Glad that you'll make something positive out of your past, out of a situation you had no control over that wasn't your fault.'

Xavier hesitated, stunned at how intuitively she'd touched a nerve.

'It doesn't mean I forgive him,' he said, bluntly. He doubted he'd ever be able to do that. 'But our baby has given me a reason to think about the importance of heritage. Just because I wish I wasn't related to de la Rosa, doesn't mean my child will feel the same way. He or she deserves the chance to make their own decisions about all of this. About who he or she is and where they belong. Don't you think?'

Lola watched him, blinking, her eyes shining with emotion. 'I guess... Although it's a pretty intimidating legacy for one so small.' She rested her hand over her belly as if their child needed protecting from the enormity of all this, which he guessed it did.

Xavier swallowed and glanced away pretending to find his paella fascinating when, in reality, his appetite had vanished to be replaced by doubts. What the hell did he know about being a father? But just like he would take viticulture classes to learn about wine, he could also learn about parenthood.

'So… How are we going to tackle this situation?' he asked quietly.

Lola sighed and his stomach knotted with dread. She wasn't ready to talk about the details, he'd sensed that. But he needed to plan, to think about logistics like baby-proofing the house and beefing up estate security.

'We're both mature, responsible people,' she said, evenly. 'I think we can figure things out, don't you?'

'I hope so.' He glanced down at his barely touched food. 'I… It goes without saying, but I want to be fully involved.' He met her stare, his heart pounding, his body rigid with contained feelings. 'I want to be a better father than he was.'

Lola smiled softly, tilted her head and reached out her hand, covering his. 'That wouldn't be hard. For what it's worth, I think you're going to be an amazing father. Our baby will be lucky to have you.'

That she hadn't dismissed his fears made his respect for her soar through the roof. That she saw him capable of loving their child, choked him to the point of breathlessness. How could she be so certain? He wasn't. He knew he would protect the child with his life, that he'd try to ensure that it was happy and healthy and had every opportunity in life, but what if the love didn't come? What if he'd spent so long shutting people out, uncertain of who he could trust with his feelings, guarding them against rejection and betrayal, that he was incapable of love? What if deep down, he was more like de la Rosa than he knew?

'I don't know what I'm doing,' he said, his doubts so huge, they made a verbal bid for freedom. 'But I want to be there, which is why I wanted you to stay here in Castilona.'

She nodded, falling silent.

'That being said,' he went on, 'if you do permanently move back to Spain, then I'll move there too. I can leave all of this to manage itself, as de la Rosa did, and help you to raise the baby...if that's okay?'

Lola nodded, her stare shining. 'That's fine by me, Xavier. But we have plenty of time. We don't have to decide right now where we'll end up living, do we?'

Xavier shook his head and she relaxed, began eating, while he felt light-headed with relief and doubt, because everything was still up in the air. But he wouldn't push her any more tonight. He would feed her then take her home and try his best not to kiss her goodnight. Because the only constant in his life at the moment, the only thing he could rely upon, was that around her, he was consumed by burning need.

CHAPTER NINE

USING AN ESTATE vehicle rather than his personal one to avoid being followed by the paps, Xavier had driven Lola home. After such an emotional evening, she hoped that a warm shower before bed would lull her into a restful sleep, one where she slept through any erotic dreams about Xavier. She'd just pulled on her favourite silk pyjamas when the buzzer to her apartment sounded, jarringly.

Lola hurried to the intercom near the door, fear clutching at her throat. Who would be on her doorstep at this time of night? The couple of female friends she'd made in Castilona would only call this late if it was something urgent. Perhaps Xavier had forgotten something after dropping her home.

Seeing a dark male figure she didn't recognise on the security screen, she warily pressed the intercom. 'Yes?'

'Dr Garcia, I wondered if you would give an interview to *Estilo Magazine*? I can pay you for your time, but we'd love to do a feature on your relationship with the new *Marqués de Moro*.'

Lola gasped, rearing away from the intercom in shock. She stepped backwards as if physical distance would erase this from reality. How had they found her? Had someone at the hospital leaked her home address? And what did they want? She had no intention of talking to anyone.

Ignoring the man, Lola moved to the window and peeked through the blinds, gasping once more as she saw the group of paps on the street, looking perfectly at ease. Chatting, sipping takeaway coffee and chain smoking as if they planned to spend the night camped outside her apartment block.

The man who'd rung the bell leaned on the button so the buzzer sounded continuously, making her jump as it echoed around the otherwise silent room. She had no personal experience of this. She was an ordinary woman. Yes she'd managed the press as part of her role at the clinic, but this was different. Intrusive. Threatening. And if they could find out where she lived, when her and Xavier weren't even a couple, what would stop them finding out about the baby?

She dropped a protective hand to her abdomen. Then with trembling fingers, she called Xavier.

He answered after a single ring. 'Are you okay?'

She winced at the panic in his voice, feeling silly for calling so late. 'I'm fine. But there are journalists and paparazzi on my doorstep. I don't know what to do.' The one who'd knocked continued to press the buzzer so she put her finger in her ear so she could hear Xavier over the horrible sound.

'Don't answer the door,' he said, his voice firm but calm, making her feel instantly better. 'I'll be there in ten minutes.'

'No... I'm fine.' She back-pedalled. It wasn't as if she was in any danger, although she'd never be able to sleep through that noise. And would they still be there in the morning when she left for work? 'I was just on my way to bed but I doubt I'll be able to sleep now, especially as one of them hasn't stopped pressing my doorbell. Can you hear it?'

'You can come back here,' he said, his voice breathless as if he was running while he spoke.

'There's no need for that,' Lola said. 'What do they even want from me? How did they even find me?'

'They must have followed us when I dropped you home. I'm sorry. I thought we'd lost them.'

'Should I call the police?' she asked, her paranoia building.

'I'll be with you in eight minutes,' he said, obviously driving now.

'Okay,' she said in a voice that sounded far too small for her liking.

'Pack an overnight bag,' he said. 'You won't

be disturbed at Casa Colina and I can keep them away from you there.'

When she hesitated and said nothing he went on. 'You've seen the layout. You can take any of the bedrooms you like. Even in the guest house you'll be safe.'

Lola glanced around her small apartment, stacked with moving boxes. She'd once loved this place, but now it felt tainted somehow. As if she'd been burgled, her possessions rifled.

'Don't speed,' she said, heading to the bedroom and taking out her overnight bag from the closet. 'There's an underground garage. The code is six-three-eight-seven. They won't be able to follow you there.' She threw some work clothes, underwear, toiletries and her toothbrush into the bag.

'Don't count on it,' he said bitterly. 'You won't believe the lengths some of them went to just to get a shot of Princess Xiomara.'

While Xavier stayed on the line, Lola quickly changed out of her pyjamas into jeans and a sweatshirt, slipping on her comfiest ballet flats.

'I'm pulling into the garage now,' he said. 'Stay in your apartment. I'll come up and meet you.'

She topped up Albie's food and water, although she knew the cat sitter would do that too, and when she finally opened the door to Xavier, having verified his presence through the peep hole, she almost sagged into his arms with relief. She prided herself on being a strong, independent, capable woman, but being pregnant made her feel more vulnerable somehow. As if she was keeping two lives safe, which she was.

Taking her bag, Xavier rested his hand on her shoulder. 'Have you got everything you need?'

Suddenly his intimidating height, his physique and training and calm assurance filled her with confidence. She nodded.

'Lock up,' he instructed, 'and let's go.'

With her hand gripping his, she followed him to the garage. They made it to the car without incident, but as the electronic grill-style exit gate raised and they pulled out onto the street, the car was swarmed by paps all pointing their cameras at the windows and yelling their names.

Lola sank down into the passenger seat, her heart pounding with adrenaline, her first instinct to cover her face.

'It's okay,' Xavier soothed, steering single handedly so he could reach for her hand and squeeze it. 'I won't let them get anywhere near you.'

Not hesitating for a second, Xavier drove away, leaving the paps to scramble, jumping onto mopeds and giving chase. Xavier drove as if they weren't there, confident in the features of his modified luxury car—driver attention monitor, tinted bulletproof glass and a three hundred and sixty degree camera system.

It was only when they'd finally pulled through

the double automatic gate system back at Casa Colina that Lola was able to breathe easy.

Xavier's entire body remained tense as he ushered Lola inside, fury boiling through him that they'd gone after her to get to him.

In the hallway, he gripped her shoulders and scanned her from head to toe. 'Are you okay?'

Choked by fear, he wanted to ask about the baby but couldn't. He wanted to drag her into his arms and hold her until the panicked pounding of his heart had eased. He wanted to dedicate the rest of his life to making sure she and their child were safe. But he was acting crazy and getting ahead of himself. Lola hated being fussed over.

'I'm fine,' she said, looking pale and tired. 'I was just shocked. Sorry if I worried you.'

He dropped his hands from her shoulders, not trusting himself to drag her into his arms and never let her leave. 'I'd rather you were here, where there's a wall and security gates to keep people out.'

'Thank you. For rescuing me,' she said attempting a smile. Then she stepped forward and embraced him, her arms around his waist and her head on his chest.

Xavier froze, one hand between her shoulder blades, the other at his side holding onto her overnight bag. His body reacting to her closeness and how right she felt in his arms with her heart beating against his. For a dangerously indulgent second, he dipped his head and inhaled the scent of her shampoo, closing his eyes as the desire he'd been denying all these long weeks since the storm rushed through him, like fizz from an uncorked bottle.

Using all his strength, every scrap of his discipline, he stepped back. If he didn't put some walls between them soon, he might do something stupid. He wasn't trying to seduce her. He needed to protect her and their baby. He wanted them to work on a respectful and mature relationship as parents. That had to be his priority.

'Would you prefer the guest house,' he asked, 'or one of the rooms upstairs?'

Lola frowned as if upset he'd ended their embrace. But she surely didn't want to reopen that closed door, did she? Not when things were so much more complicated between them now compared to the night of the storm.

She crossed her arms as if she was cold. 'Where do you sleep? I… I'd feel safer in a guest room in the main house if that's okay.'

Maybe she just wanted comfort. She must be spooked by what had happened tonight.

'Of course it is,' he said, wondering how in the hell he'd manage to sleep with her so close by. 'I'm on the first floor, one of the smaller rooms you looked into earlier. Why don't you take the master bedroom? It's at the end of the hall, so I won't disturb you, and you won't be alone in the guest wing, which by the way is perfectly safe and fitted with the same alarm system as the rest of the house but feels…lonely I guess.'

Lola nodded gratefully, relaxing slightly. 'Okay. Thank you.'

With his mind full of plans to increase security at Casa Colina, Xavier showed her the way to the master bedroom, a room he'd rejected for himself. One because he was a simple guy with simple needs and two because he'd guessed that de la Rosa had used it once. Even though he'd had it redecorated when he'd first moved in, purchasing brand new furniture, he still preferred the smaller room.

On the threshold, he passed over her bag. 'I'm right down the hall if you need anything. There's also an intercom beside the bed, which connects to Tia, the housekeeper, if you want a drink or something to eat.'

Lola shook her head, her eyes dark and haunted in the dim light of the room's lamps. 'I won't need anything, but thanks.' She stared, as if she might say more but didn't.

Swallowing down the turmoil inside him—the lingering fear for her safety, the arousal from holding her, the innate need to do the honourable thing—he forced himself to step back. 'Sleep well. See you in the morning. I'll take you to work.'

His stare swept over her one final time, then he

headed downstairs to his office where he placed a series of calls to some recently discharged army buddies he would trust with his life, offering them a salary they couldn't refuse to join the estate's security.

Safety was his job, and the one thing he could do for Lola and his child, and he intended to do it to the best of his ability.

CHAPTER TEN

BY THE END of the week, after Lola had been sleeping at Casa Colina for a few days, Xavier was certain that he was losing his mind. Having her there, driving her to work every day, sharing breakfast or dinner with her, reassured him that she and the baby were safe. But his peace of mind came at a high price. He was just about ready to crawl out of his skin with sexual frustration. He wanted her. Ached for her. Awoke from dreams where he was either searching the house for her in vain or rolling around naked with her, their passion for each other obliterating everything he stood for in life. There seemed to be no reprieve from the way being around her made him feel...unstable. And he had no idea what to do about it.

Glancing up from his laptop in the cool of the air-conditioned library, he spied her out by the pool and muttered a curse under his breath. Dressed in one of those long, flowing sun dresses she liked to wear when she was off duty, her shapely figure and slim legs visible through the sheer fabric, which was virtually see-through in the sunlight, made his mouth water.

The only thing worse than that torture, was when she donned a worn pair of cut-off denim shorts, pairing them with a simple white tank top that left him in no doubt that she was braless beneath, her breasts fuller than he remembered and nipples poking through the fabric, as if begging for his attention.

He looked away with a snort of self-disgust, trying to return his focus to the spreadsheet before him. But the numbers, a balance sheet of expenditure and profit predictions for the coming wine growing season, swam before his eyes, which once more sought out Lola.

'*Dios...*' he muttered, seeing that she'd now removed the filmy dress to reveal a sexy black bikini, the tiny triangles of fabric barely covering her gorgeous breasts and the haven between her legs. The small swell of her abdomen called to that primal part of him that needed to protect her and his child. If he hadn't memorised her body's shape from the night of the storm, obsessing over the images he'd stored like a fanatic, he doubted he'd be able to tell that she was pregnant.

Before drool could leave the corner of his mouth, Lola dived into the pool, sinking from his view, gifting him a few moments of respite from the hell in which he was trapped. Instead of returning to estate business, he checked the property's security camera feeds, all eighteen of them, which covered the walled and fenced perimeter of the property, every entrance and exit and the first and ground floor hallways.

Unsatisfied with what he saw, which was nothing more than another stunning Castilonian spring day, he picked up the walkie talkie and radioed the security team he'd employed the day after Lola had moved in.

'Status update,' he said, knowing his ex-army colleagues would think nothing of his abruptness. They, like him, understood the world in a way that most people were insulated from.

'All clear at the front,' one guard, Carlos, responded.

'Rear secure too, over,' the other, Marco, replied.

Xavier tried to console himself with their reassurance, but ever since the night he'd rescued Lola from the paparazzi on her street, he just couldn't seem to relax. Ever.

'Mrs Torres will be arriving shortly,' he told Carlos who was manning the front gate. 'Please let me know when she gets here.'

He'd invited his mother for dinner so he could introduce Lola and tell Carlota about the baby. After another ten minutes of fruitless work, Xavier abandoned his laptop and headed for the kitchen, where Tia was busy preparing a dinner of *albondigas*—Spanish meatballs in a garlic and tomato sauce, *patatas bravas* and a Mediterranean salad.

'Mr Torres,' she chided as he opened the cabinet, retrieved a water glass and filled it with ice from the fridge. 'If you tell me what you need, I will bring it to you, sir.'

'Please call me Xavier, Tia. And while I appreciate everything you do here, I have legs. I can fetch my own glass of water.' He doubted he'd ever become accustomed to having someone do things for him.

The older woman, a widow with two university-aged children, tilted her head in a way that told him he'd won this skirmish, but the war would be protracted and fiercely fought.

'My mother is on her way,' he told her. 'I'll warn you now that she has never once visited me empty handed, so please don't be offended if she brings enough food to feed the entire estate.'

'Her cooking is legendary.' Tia smiled. 'I hope to part her from some of her famous, well-guarded palace recipes.' Tia's smile widened, her stare landing on someone over Xavier's shoulder.

Xavier turned, already certain it was Lola from the light floral scent of her perfume and the uncontrollable quickening of his pulse.

'Nice swim?' he asked, noting that she'd changed into another floaty dress that showed off her gorgeous figure. Her hair looked freshly blow dried and she'd scooped it into a casual top knot he wanted to undo while he buried his face against her neck.

'Blissful,' she said, helping herself to an olive from the bowl Tia had set next to a sweating jug of home-made lemonade. 'Dinner smells delicious, Tia. I'm ravenous.'

Giving his hands something to do that wasn't touch Lola and satisfy her other appetites, Xavier collected the tray of lemonade and suggested they sit in the conservatory to wait for Carlota.

'I wanted to ask you,' he said carefully, 'if I can tell my mother about the baby tonight? I can't risk her finding out from the media. I hope that's okay.'

Lola nodded, looking a little guilty. 'Of course. That's fine by me. I just... I hope she understands.' She licked her lips nervously.

Xavier glanced at her hand, fighting the urge to hold it. 'That we're not a couple?' he asked instead, the unease that had rumbled inside him since he'd discovered that Lola was having his baby increasing because while they'd agreed in principle to raise this baby together, they had none of the finer details planned. Whatever Lola's plans turned out to be, the estate was entering its busy season with the vines full of spring growth and the cellar door open for tastings and sales of previous years' vintages. It would take some planning for him to follow her if she decided to head back to Spain, permanently.

'Yes,' she said. 'I hope she understands that we didn't plan this. That I didn't set out to trap you or something...'

'Please don't worry,' Xavier said. 'She was a single parent herself. I guarantee she'll be delighted by the news. Although I might be scolded in private for being...careless.'

Discussing the moment they'd conceived, inevitably brought erotic memories flooding in. Had he ever connected so fully with a woman? The desire for her was becoming increasingly persistent. It might actually kill him.

'You weren't careless,' Lola said, looking at him in that way of hers—with intelligence and intuition, as if she saw through him to the places even he was scared to probe. 'I used to be on birth control, but I haven't dated for two years and I hadn't planned on sleeping with you. And I get the occasional migraine so didn't want to take unnecessary medication.'

Hearing her talk about her dating life only increased his restlessness. 'Did you want a child eventually?' he asked cautiously. Since she'd moved in, they'd avoided discussing the practicalities, but they each knew that conversation loomed.

'Yes. My family are very close,' she said. 'My parents are still wildly in love even after forty years of marriage. What about you?'

Xavier swallowed, unused to discussing his

feelings. 'I've never had a relationship serious enough to give it any thought.'

'Not ever?' she asked, her intelligent stare appraising him.

'No. Like you I've been focussed on my career. Focussed on building a secure life for myself, living with my vision limitations.' Letting someone get close came with risk and he'd had enough rejection to last a lifetime, thanks to de la Rosa.

Just then, the radio he'd taken to wearing on his waistband crackled to life. 'Señora Torres has arrived, sir.'

'Thank you,' Xavier replied then stood. 'Ready?' he asked Lola, who ran a nervous hand over the escaped wisps of her hair and nodded. 'Don't be nervous.' He swept his gaze over her. 'You look beautiful. She's going to love you.'

Xavier headed outside to meet the car, Lola at his side. Knowing that Carlota rarely followed celebrity gossip, all he'd told her was that a friend from work had come to stay at Casa Colina. As soon as he'd mentioned Lola's name, and Carlota discovered the friend was a woman, her voice had turned high pitched with hope. He'd never lived with a woman before, nor introduced Carlota to anyone he dated.

When Carlota climbed from her car, he made introductions. As he'd known she would, Carlota warmly embraced Lola as if they were old friends. While Xavier carried in the two foil-covered plates from the back seat, Carlota looped her arm through Lola's as they walked back inside, already chatting about the weather, dinner and the amazing views from the house.

With everyone once more seated in the sun room, and after a brief period of small talk where Carlota asked Lola about her work and her family, Xavier cleared his throat.

'Mamá, I have some news,' he said, glancing Lola's way, catching her small nod of encouragement. 'Lola and I are having a child.'

Carlota gasped, her hand reaching for Lola's arm as her eyes filled with the shine of tears. 'Really? Is it true?'

Lola nodded, blinking with emotion. 'Yes. We have the first scan next week, but I think I'm almost eight weeks along.'

Carlota threw her arms around Lola's neck and hugged her. Then, standing, she embraced Xavier tighter than he ever remembered being hugged.

'Don't get too excited,' he warned, sliding another glance Lola's way. 'We're not actually dating or together. It just…happened. The night of Cyclone Gabriel.'

Carlota waved her hand dismissively. 'I don't care how or when. I'm just delighted. But how are you feeling, *amado*?' she asked Lola, retaking her seat.

Lola glanced at Xavier and smiled. 'I'm fine. A little more tired than usual, but otherwise good.'

'And you're getting plenty of rest?' Carlota pushed, casting him a look he easily interpreted—*take care of her*.

'It's wonderfully relaxing here,' Lola said. 'I'm very comfortable and have been enjoying swimming in the pool after work.'

Carlota nodded with enthusiasm. 'So have you told your family? Are they planning to visit?'

Xavier winced. This was the tricky part. The details that he and Lola had yet to discuss and agree on.

'I've told my twin sister, Isla,' Lola said. 'But my parents will also be delighted to be grandparents.'

'Good.' Carlota clapped her hands together. 'I'm so happy for you both and for myself of course. An *abuela* at last.'

The women beamed at one another. Xavier stiffened, his doubts returning. Surely he and Lola could successfully navigate parenthood in a mature and respectful way. He'd have to make it work. He couldn't afford to mess this up because he'd have the most to lose.

Just then, there was a cry from the kitchen. Lola's startled stare shot to Xavier's. They both stood, hurrying into the other room to find Tia standing over the kitchen sink, her hand wrapped in a towel.

'Oh, Mr Torres, I'm so sorry,' she said. 'The knife slipped and I've cut my hand. So careless.' She winced at all three of them, her cheeks flushed with embarrassment.

'Tia, please don't worry,' Xavier said. 'How bad is it? Let us see.'

Tia gingerly unwrapped the towel, her cupped palm instantly filling with a pool of blood.

'Sit down,' he told her, quickly reapplying the towel and exerting pressure while he steered Tia over to a chair.

'I think it's going to need stitches,' Lola said once she'd examined the wound, looking up at Xavier over the top of Tia's head.

'I'll drive you to the hospital,' Xavier said, collecting more towels from the drawer.

'No,' Tia wailed. 'Your dinner...your mother.' She glanced at Carlota who was near the door, keeping out of the way. 'Please do not trouble yourself over me.' Tia stood but Xavier pushed her gently back down. The last thing they needed was her passing out and hitting her head.

'I have a suture kit in my medical bag,' Lola said. 'If you want, I can do it here. But you must attend the accident department at St Sebastian's tomorrow for a tetanus shot and some antibiotics,' she told Tia, who nodded meekly.

Lola met Xavier's stare. 'My bag is in the closet of my room.'

'I'll get it.' Xavier rushed to fetch it and when he returned, the three women had moved to the sink in the downstairs cloakroom.

'Let me take over with compression,' Xavier said, once he'd washed his hands and pulled on some gloves. He applied pressure to the wound while Lola also washed up and pulled on gloves.

Just like the night of the storm when she'd sutured up the wound to Maria Fernandez's head, she and Xavier worked together now while Carlota left the room, returning to the kitchen to remove dinner from the oven.

Lola injected local anaesthetic around the cut while Xavier did his best to staunch the bleeding.

'Don't worry,' Xavier playfully told Tia, 'I've seen Dr Garcia do this before. She's very neat with the stitches.'

Lola smiled at them both, her eyes lingering on Xavier. Something like respect shone in her stare as if she was grateful for his presence, just as she'd been the night of the storm.

'I'm so embarrassed that I ruined dinner,' Tia said.

'Are you kidding?' Xavier said softly, trying to take her mind off the procedure going on. 'My mother's probably out there right now adding the finishing touches. She's only happy when she's in a kitchen and she'd have inserted herself into the preparations one way or another.'

Tia smiled at him and touched his arm. 'You're a good man Mr Torres. Thank you for coming to Casa Colina. Your energy has changed the place and let in more sunlight. All the staff are happy.'

Feeling Lola's eyes on him, Xavier stiffened, unused to compliments.

Lola, busy placing a neat row of sutures to close the wound, didn't seem to notice that his chest felt too small for his lungs. In the few short weeks he'd lived there, he'd come to know every one of the staff the estate employed. How de la Rosa had inspired such loyalty, he had no idea, but he considered himself honoured to know these kind-hearted, hard-working people.

While he tried to pull himself together, Lola covered the wound with a sterile dressing. 'There. All done.'

She met his stare and he looked away, feeling raw. 'No more work for you tonight,' Xavier told Tia, who looked like she might argue.

'Take some painkillers,' Lola said. 'And get some rest. If you shower, pop your hand into a plastic bag to keep the dressing dry.'

When Tia hesitated, looking as if she wanted to clean up the bathroom before she retired to her rooms, they shooed her off together.

'I'll ask Mamá to bring you a plate of whatever smells so good in the kitchen,' Xavier said.

'Thank you, Mr Torres. Dr Garcia,' Tia said as she left the room.

When they were alone, he and Lola set to cleaning up.

'She's right you know,' she said quietly about Tia, placing the equipment she'd used into a sealed biohazard bag and a small portable sharps bin. 'I know you didn't ask for all this, but you're a natural at leading people. You're fair, compassionate and down to earth. Having met your lovely mother tonight, I can understand why. She adores you.'

Xavier stiffened, his pulse leaping, the urge to pull her into his arms and hold her until everything made sense, stronger than ever before. What she and Tia had said was compliment enough. But the words they hadn't said were even more devastating because what he'd heard was *you're nothing like him*.

'You're pretty good with people yourself,' he said gruffly, placing the soiled towels in a rubbish bag. If he didn't leave her company soon, he was going to do something they might both regret and with so much at stake—the baby, their relationship as parents, the future—he needed a clear head.

Lola smiled as she sprayed down the vanity with disinfectant spray. 'We do make a good team.'

It was true. But more than that, their chemistry, his near constant need for her, just wouldn't be silenced. They left the tied-up rubbish bag and Lola's medical bag in the laundry, and washed their hands at the sink.

'I'll help your mother finish dinner,' she said, her smile taking him back to the night of the storm.

'Good luck with that.' Xavier replied, doubtful that the ravenous hunger in him could be satiated by food alone.

CHAPTER ELEVEN

Lola startled awake. Someone was gently shaking her shoulder. Gasping, she opened her eyes to find Xavier leaning over her in the gloom of the darkened living room.

'It's okay,' he said. 'Just me.'

His hand fell away from her shoulder and she almost cried out, her body eagerly craving his touch, as it had since that night of the storm.

'I fell asleep,' she said instead, sitting up, taking a moment to recover from her disorientation.

Xavier had left thirty minutes ago to drive Carlota home. Lola had checked on Tia then sat down with a book to wait for his return. After Tia's accident, he'd been quiet throughout dinner, barely eating a thing. She wanted to make sure he was okay. After all, he was used to having his own space. He'd insisted she stay there, but maybe he was struggling, because things seemed to be moving so fast—the house, the baby, them living together.

But no matter how often she told herself it

would be a mistake to submit to her need for him, it beat at her in relentless waves. Each look, each touch, each considerate thing he did for her weakening her resolve. Xavier, on the other hand, seemed oblivious as if he'd well and truly moved on.

'Sorry to wake you,' he said, stepping back, his posture rigid. 'I didn't want to leave you here all night.' His eyes were almost black in the dim light from the lamp, his body tense as if coiled with energy.

'Was Carlota okay?' she asked, sitting on the edge of the sofa. She felt wary of him because ever since she'd moved in, her hand forced by the persistent paps, there'd been a weird forcefield between them, binding them somehow but also creating an emotional distance she didn't like. It made sense. For her their chemistry was still exhaustingly intense, but Xavier was an expert at keeping her out and personally they had a lot to discuss.

'She chatted about the baby all the way home,' he said, his voice indulgent. 'It's not even born yet and she's already going through her family, suggesting names for us to consider.'

'She's lovely,' Lola said, feeling closer to him now that she'd met Carlota, who clearly adored her son and had raised him to be the strong, capable, selfless man he was. 'I couldn't have wished for a better *abuela* for our baby. She's clearly very proud of you.'

Xavier shrugged. 'I'm an only child. There's no one else for her to focus on.'

He was deflecting, clearly uncomfortable with compliments.

'She'd be proud of you if she had a hundred children.' Lola stood stretching out her back and shoulders, which were stiff from falling asleep on the sofa.

When Xavier's gaze dropped to her breasts, which she'd accidentally thrust out, she froze, keen anticipation and excitement flooding her body.

'Why didn't you go to bed?' he asked, not moving away, his intense stare hooded.

'I wanted to make sure you were okay,' she admitted. 'You were quiet tonight. More so than usual.' She offered him a small smile, but her heart wasn't in it. She felt too volatile, strung out on the way he made her feel both safe and reckless in the same heartbeat. But wanting him was more dangerous than before. They were living together. They had the baby to consider. They had a future to plan.

'You waited up for me?' he asked, gruffly, adding no further explanation of his strange mood.

'I tried…' She said with a shrug and another half-hearted smile. Her expression slipped because, danger or not, something had shifted between them, making her heart flutter erratically and her stomach hollow with fear and longing, as if what happened next was vital—a crossroads.

'You should go up to bed,' he said, making no move to leave, his intense stare shifting over her face as his breathing sped up, as if he too was waiting for something to happen and was unable to walk away.

Lola sighed, certain that he felt it too, this building pressure they'd danced around and dodged for the past few weeks, since the storm.

'Are *you* going up?' she asked, her body swaying towards his.

Even as she craved him, desperation making heat pool in her belly and between her legs, she couldn't stop herself from challenging him, testing him, pushing him for more.

'Not tired yet,' he said, his fingers twitching at his sides as if he wanted to touch her, to kiss her. As if he could read her mind. Then his tongue darted out to swipe at his lip.

Lola moaned silently, recalling the brush of that clever tongue over her skin, her nipples, her clit. Excitement energised her. She wanted him. Surely they were mature enough to navigate both sex and sharing a home while keeping feelings off the table. Xavier excelled at the latter and she could handle herself.

'You know I always do what I want, not what I'm told,' she said, boldly stepping closer, because he was too far away and she was full of hormones and only he could appease her neediness.

'Lola...' he warned, his voice a low rumble, his facial muscles bunching as he clenched his jaw. But he held his ground, his breath gusting through flared nostrils as he stared her down.

She was playing with fire. But if she had to stay in his home while also carrying their child, had to see him every day both at home and work, there ought to be some payback. It was only fair.

'I'm turned on,' she said, her breaths coming short and fast. 'You made me pregnant and now I'm a slave to my hormones. You invite me to live with you, dangling yourself in front of me like a forbidden snack. What are you going to do about it, Xavier?'

She'd never done well with self-denial. If she wanted something, she made it happen. And she wanted him. Now. Tonight. A reprieve from this tension that had pulled taut to snapping point.

'Ignore it,' he said in a low voice. 'That's the sensible thing to do.' But he leaned closer, as if he couldn't stop himself. As if he wanted her too just as much.

'I've tried since the night of the storm,' she said, 'and it's no longer working.' She took another step closer until she felt the warm gusts of his breath brush over her parted lips. Felt the heat of his body bathe her in his scent. Felt the delicious anticipation in the way he held back. 'If we have to be under the same roof, it makes sense that we shouldn't have to suffer. I'm tired of fighting. It's just sex. We moved on from it before. We can do it again.'

She raised her gaze from his mouth to his dark, unreadable eyes. But this time, she saw what he was trying so hard to conceal—fire, desperation, barely contained restraint.

'We agreed on one night,' he said, showing his superior mental strength, as if he was desperate to do the right thing.

'Minds are for changing,' she whispered, certain that she couldn't go another day in denial.

'Lola...' he groaned, panting hard now, clearly struggling, wavering, torn. He curled his hands into fists at his side.

'Xavier,' she moaned, reaching for his wrists, bringing his hands up to her tingling breasts. 'Touch me,' she begged. 'I'm achy and it's all your fault.'

When he did as she asked, she bit down on her lip and sighed. Only he could put her out of her misery. Only this, them taking what had begun the night of the storm and harnessing it, made sense.

With another groan of defeat, he dragged her into his arms. His hands spread over her ribcage as he lowered his mouth to hers in a fierce kiss that filled her with electrifying triumph. She parted her lips and met the surges of his tongue with her own. Clinging to his neck to keep her body pressed to his, desperate to find as much contact and as much friction and heat as possible. She wanted to burn, safe in his arms, knowing he'd not only take her there, but also catch her as she fell apart.

'Yes,' she cried, dropping her head back to give his mouth access to her neck as his hand slid the strap of her sun dress from her shoulder.

He cupped her bare breast, his thumb brushing over her sensitive nipple, spreading tingles throughout her body, adding to her desperation. Her fingernails dug into his upper arms as she clung to him, willing him to continue, needing his touch as much as she needed air. Wanting to break him because his mere presence had broken every one of her good intentions.

'You're sure this is what you want?' he asked, his arm banded around her waist so she felt his erection against her stomach while that thumb rubbed and teased. Desire darkened his eyes to black.

'Yes,' she cried, eyes wide open, her body restless against his. 'Positive.'

He cupped her chin, raised her face, lowered his stare to her half-naked chest. 'You wore that bikini on purpose today, didn't you?' he said, impatiently raising her breast to his mouth, his tongue lashing the peak over and over in punishment until her legs almost buckled.

She gripped his biceps to hold herself up, riding his hard thigh to try and appease the viscous throb between her legs. 'I knew you were watching,' she said on a moan. 'I felt your eyes on me.'

'Did you want my eyes on you?' he asked, sliding one hand under her dress and along her thigh.

'Yes,' she said, shoving at the hem of his black t-shirt until he removed it, desperate to see him naked once more. 'I want it all.'

Denied his sublime body since the storm, Lola pressed kisses to his chest, her hands caressing his flexed abs, her nails lightly scoring his muscular back, her skin picking up the gorgeous scent of him. She covered his nipple with her mouth, laving and sucking as he'd done to her until he groaned, walked her back towards the sofa and pulled her down astride his lap as he sat.

'I've wanted this every day, since the storm.' He peeled down the other strap of her dress, exposing her from the waist up, his stare devouring her nakedness. 'Are you sensitive?' he asked, cupping her breasts, toying with the nipples, leaning down to capture one with his lips and stroke it with his hot tongue.

'A little,' she moaned, thrusting her chest forward. 'It's wonderful. Don't stop.'

He rubbed one nipple harder, his tongue laving the other. Gasping in delight, Lola rocked on his lap. Seeking the friction of his hard length between her legs and frustrated by the barrier of his jeans and her underwear.

'Xavier, I need you,' she begged, uncaring that he'd hear the desperation in her voice. This chemistry had been between them from the start. Now, when she was living in his house and carrying his baby, was no time to deny it. But just because they were acting on it, didn't mean either of them wanted more than sex.

He leaned back, peering up at her with desire, his hands sliding up her thighs under her dress. She rocked her hips, unable to keep still with him looking at her as if he wanted to devour her. His fingers brushed her clit through her underwear and she moaned. She closed her eyes as he slipped them inside the lacy barrier to where she was unashamedly soaking wet for him.

'Don't stop,' she said, biting her lower lip as he stroked her and pleasure streaked like lightning down her legs and up to her nipples.

'Look at me, Lola,' he said, pushing his fingers inside her while his thumb kept on brushing her clit, over and over so her muscles clenched around him.

Lola did as he'd asked, her hands braced on his shoulders. Their stares locked as he took her higher and higher, his other hand on her hips to hold her firm. But she was going nowhere. This had been building between them since that first night, as if they had unfinished business and needed some sort of physical closure.

Collapsing forward, she kissed him, wildly riding his hand as he held her in his strong arm. His thighs steel beneath her bottom. His groans encouraging her to take what she needed.

Her orgasm came swiftly, her muscles gripping his fingers and her cries ringing out through the silent house as the unbearable tension finally eased.

When she was spent, he removed his hand from between her legs, encouraged her to stand on her shaky legs and stripped her naked. His dark stare touching every part of her body, the way it had that first time, as if he couldn't look away.

'Do you want me to use a condom?' he asked, his voice thick with lust. 'I'm tested regularly.'

'No,' she said, a ghost of a smile tugging at her lips. 'That horse has kind of already bolted.' Then because he had too many clothes on and she was naked, she dropped to her knees between his spread thighs and unzipped his jeans where he sat. He raised his hips and together they removed his jeans and boxers. He groaned low in the back of his throat and cupped her face when she took him into her mouth, ruthlessly pleasuring him, sucking him the way he'd done to her that time in the shower. She hummed, enjoying the way his fingers curled into her hair as he watched, the soft grunts of pleasure he made, the way every muscle in his body had turned as hard as marble, as if he was clinging to his control by his fingernails and she'd put him there.

Then, as if he'd reached his limit, he pushed her away, scooped his arm around her waist and dragged her under his big powerful body on the sofa.

For a few seconds, their eyes locked, their hearts banged together, their breaths mingling as they panted. Lola burned everywhere their skin touched, that fire centring once more between her legs as he slowly pushed inside her, filling her up. She gasped, smiling at his long-awaited possession. He groaned, his face twisting in agonising rapture as he held himself still, as deeply as possible. Because she wanted more, Lola crossed her ankles in the small of his back and he sank lower, deeper, right where she needed him, where she ached anew.

'Xavier,' she whispered, cupping his face, spearing her fingers through his damp hair to drag his mouth down to hers.

His kisses began slow, his tongue thrusting inside her mouth as his hips moved shallowly at first.

'Don't hold back,' she said against his ear when they'd come up for air. Just because she was pregnant didn't make her fragile, nor did it lessen her overwhelming desire for him. In fact, it made it stronger.

He reared up on his forearms, his lips capturing her nipple once more. Pleasure boiled in her pelvis, spreading, burning, making her gasp and moan as he thrust faster and deeper, finally giving her what she'd craved all this time.

'Xavier,' she cried, letting him know that she was close again as she clung to his shoulders and spread her legs wider.

With a harsh groan from him and a cry from her, they came together, crushing each other, their hearts thundering in harmony so it seemed as if they were one being, not two, each needing the other to survive.

But as good as they were together, Lola also clung to their limitations. They weren't a couple. He'd never needed a serious relationship or love. She needed her independence and had almost made a catastrophic mistake once before. She needed to keep sight of what this was, because neither of them wanted to ruin what they could have as parents or end up hurt.

After a few seconds, Xavier withdrew and stood, his chest still heaving, his eyes still dark with impressive desire. Then he scooped her up from the sofa and carried her upstairs to the master bedroom, the night obviously nowhere near over, much to Lola's relief.

CHAPTER TWELVE

A WEEK LATER, Xavier awoke hard, his naked body curved around Lola's as early morning light filtered through the gauzy drapes. His heart accelerated, the confusing mix of arousal and fear ensnaring him. Every day since they'd finally reached their limit of endurance and denial and found each other again, began this way. Him waking, reaching for her as if automatically, then recalling all the reasons why he couldn't get used to such an astounding start to the day.

It was just sex. Incredible, addictive sex. The infatuation would fade and when it did what remained would be the most important relationship of his life. That of co-parent with the mother of his child. *That* was where he needed to focus. *That* had to be his number one priority. The thing he guarded with his life.

Beside him, Lola stirred, her hand reaching back, fingers sliding through his hair at the nape of his neck as she pulled his mouth down to hers.

Xavier cupped her full breast, toying the nipple

awake until she moaned and kissed him harder. But while his mind fought to stay in control, his body was weak for her. Taking what he needed. Connecting in a way that was beyond words.

'Xavier,' she moaned his name as his hand slid over her belly and delved between her legs to where she was already slick for him.

She tilted her hips back, pressing her gorgeous backside into his groin, so his erection nestled between her cheeks. 'Have we got time?' she asked, reaching for him, encircling him in her hand, guiding him to her entrance. 'I need you.'

Glancing at the clock, Xavier stroked her faster as he pushed inside her from behind, skin to skin. His eyes closed on a wave of euphoria as her tight heat gripped him and he lost himself. He kissed the side of her neck, his tongue tasting her skin as she raised her arm over her head and clung to his neck. The position thrust her breasts forward. He groaned, desperate to take her pert nipples into his mouth because she loved that, crying out and twisting his hair.

'Come for me,' he said, stroking her faster. His free hand cupping her breast, toying with the nipple, pushing her closer and closer.

'Yes,' she cried, tilting her hips back so he sank deeper with every thrust, the frenzy building as they each chased the pleasure they found in each other's arms.

'Need to kiss you,' he said, shifting positions

and laying on top of her, thrusting his tongue against hers as he pushed back inside her and their hearts banged together, chest to chest. Her nails dug into his shoulder. Her moans growing erratic as they chased oblivion together. Every part of them entwined—their legs, their fingers, their tongues. Then she was coming and he let go too, groaning as he joined her. Spilling himself inside her and holding her so tight he wondered if he'd ever again be able to let her go, even though he knew he would.

Later, he rested his head on her chest and she toyed with his hair. A sense of contentment, the likes of which he'd never known, washed over him in a wave.

He placed his hand on her stomach, where their baby grew, certain that this sense of belonging, impending fatherhood, was behind the way he felt. It couldn't be anything else. It couldn't be feelings for Lola. He didn't know how to do that.

He must have sighed because Lola's hand stilled in his hair. 'Are you worried about your meeting this morning?' she asked as if they had all the time in the world. Whereas in reality, they needed to get up, shower and head out for the day—her to the hospital and him to the palace.

'No,' Xavier said about his private audience with King Octavio. 'He's just a man like me. I don't want anything from him. He's astute and intelligent, so I'm certain he will see that I'm no threat.'

Of course he had reservations, but only because the nature of his relationship with their monarch, a man Xavier had known his entire life, would be...redefined. Xavier was no longer an employee, but nor did he feel like the king's cousin. And with his cruel mistreatment from Mauricio as a boy, the king might not welcome de la Rosa's illegitimate son, although the king had been the one to issue the invitation.

'Are you worried about the scan?' she pushed, as if he were made of glass and she knew his every fear. They had Lola's first antenatal appointment that afternoon.

He shrugged. He *was* worried. Terrified. But he didn't want Lola to worry.

'I'm sure everything will be fine,' he said, the secret fears he had for the baby all but choking him.

As the day approached, Xavier had felt increasingly tossed back and forth between excitement to finally see their baby and fear that something might go wrong. What if there was something amiss with the pregnancy? What if fatherhood, the life he'd begun to feel might be his destiny, was ripped away? Would he survive another upheaval of that magnitude, just at the point he was starting to feel like he finally belonged for the first time in his life? Not there at Casa Colina, which was just stone and mortar, but as a father to his child.

'I'm sure it will be too,' Lola said reassuringly. 'I'm fit and healthy and not that old.'

Xavier nodded, eager to keep his concerns hidden. 'I'll be leaving for London straight after the scan,' he reminded her. 'Princess Xiomara can see me this evening. I thought we should discuss the recent revelations of my paternity face to face.' Another relationship about to change. He'd always admired and respected the princess, but he'd also been comfortable in his role as her employee. How would she feel that her father had produced a son? That he'd left Xavier an estate and title?

'I remember,' Lola said, stroking his hair. 'It's a big couple of days for you. Meeting our baby. Old relationships changing. Finding your place in a new family.'

Xavier raised his head and looked down at her, certain that he would always struggle to think of the de la Rosa family as *his* family when he'd spent his entire life on the outside, looking in. 'I'll be back tomorrow.'

Panic crowded his chest at the thought of leaving her and the baby there all alone. 'Carlos and Marco will both be on duty tonight for anything you need.' Although he'd arranged for double the normal security, a hundred security guards couldn't make up for his personal touch. But then he needed to get used to that. He couldn't be with

Lola all the time. One day she'd want to move on and move out. She'd want another serious relationship, maybe even marry. Then his child would have a stepfather. He shuddered and she must have felt it.

'I'll be fine,' she said, gripping his face between her palms. 'Don't worry about me.'

Xavier bit his tongue, worry seemed to be the only constant in his life at the moment. That and desire for her. What was happening to him? His fear for Lola and the baby's safety was understandable under the circumstances. The paps still hounded his every move. But the few moments of peace he felt when he and Lola were intimate, didn't seem to last long enough, driving his need for her to mindless levels. Maybe his doubts about fatherhood were making him irrational. After all, he had no role model to emulate. What if he was no good at it? What if he messed up and got it wrong? Would his child forgive him or end up needing a lifetime of therapy?

Later that afternoon, after his surreal meeting at the palace, Xavier hurried to St Sebastian's to meet Lola. She'd chosen there for her antenatal care over *Clinico San Carlos*, eager to keep her pregnancy private from her work colleagues.

Xavier arrived before her and took a seat in the waiting room, his heart kicking at his ribs when she walked in moments later. He stood as she approached, thrown off balance by his strange morning and nerves over the scan. As if sensing his turmoil, Lola pressed a kiss to his cheek and sat at his side, pulling his hand into hers.

'How was your audience this morning?' she discreetly asked about his meeting with King Octavio.

Concern dulled her eyes. Was she nervous too, or could she sense how scared he was of losing control of the security he'd built around himself with all this change.

'Fine,' he said vaguely, but grateful that she'd raised a subject designed to take his mind off the impending scan. 'My cousin, I guess...' He winced, the idea of calling their monarch that, laughable. But in this setting the name served as a useful code. Only Lola would know of whom he spoke. '...he graciously welcomed me into the family and asked if there was anything he could do for me.'

Xavier was still reeling, desperately trying to keep the redefined relationships in his life at a safe distance. But keeping Lola from seeing his deepest fears was his priority.

'I'm so glad,' she said, squeezing his arm. 'You must have been nervous, but now that the first meeting since the truth emerged has occurred, next time will be easier.'

Xavier shrugged. 'I didn't know what to expect,' he said. He'd always respected their ruler, but that respect had doubled after today. 'I figured my paternity would be a shock to all concerned.'

'But you realised that it doesn't matter,' she said. 'That it in no way reflects on you.'

Unable to express his feelings as eloquently as Lola seemed to be able to do, he gripped her hand tighter. 'We talked about the upcoming wedding,' he said referring to Princess Xiomara, who would soon return to Castilona to marry Dr Edmund Butler.

She nodded encouragingly.

'He...suggested I might play a small role,' Xavier said, flattered but doubtful that the princess would want that.

'Are you reluctant?' she asked, that insight of hers once more hitting the mark.

He replied shrugging. 'I want to do anything I can to make sure the bride is happy, but...'

She leaned close, dropping her voice to a whisper. 'I understand. It will take time for you to feel like they are family, no matter how long you've known them or how welcoming they are.'

Xavier swallowed. How could she do that so... effortlessly? See the things he was feeling when he himself struggled to decipher them? But of course he would likely always struggle to feel as if he belonged with the de la Rosa family. His family had always been Carlota and now included Lola and the baby.

The speed at which that thought filled his mind,

caught him off guard. Had he let Lola so close he considered her a part of his team? She certainly had an intuitive knack of seeing parts of him he assumed were hidden from everyone. But if she understood him so well, if she saw how deep down, there must be something wrong with him, she could easily hurt him if she chose.

Just then, with that unsettling thought in his head, a nurse called Lola's name. She and Xavier followed the woman into a consulting room, where Lola was weighed and her height and blood pressure were recorded. Then they were directed into the sonogram room.

'You can leave your clothes on,' the young female sonographer said. 'Just undo your trousers and pull up your blouse.'

Lola handed Xavier her bag, loosened her clothing and lay on the bed, smiling over at him as if she had not a care in the world. Whereas he wouldn't be able to breathe easy until they saw that tiny heartbeat.

Xavier stood stiffly at her side until she encouraged him to sit in the chair provided and then reached for his hand.

'Okay,' the sonographer said, squirting gel onto Lola's lower abdomen. 'Let's see what we have.'

Xavier's fingers tightened around Lola's as the sonographer placed the probe into position. His stare was glued to the screen, which was currently an indecipherable mass of static—like an un-tuned television channel.

Lola sent him a reassuring look, but he held his breath, strung too taut to do anything other than breathe and focus on the ultrasound machine.

'So, here we go,' the sonographer said, positioning the screen so they could see the image more clearly. 'The black area is the amniotic sac and this is your baby.'

Xavier stared in wonder. The tiny human he and Lola had made easily recognisable now—head, spine, arms and legs.

Losing his breath as if winded, Xavier clung to Lola's hand. It was real. His baby existed. Would he be able to love it as he should? What if there was an inherited inability to love in him, passed on from de la Rosa? He'd always believed his lack of interest in romantic love came from his hang ups, the rejection he'd grown up with, the deep fear that *he* must be unlovable. But what if he simply couldn't love because, like it or not, he was related to that man?

'I'm just going to do some measurements to corroborate your dates.' The sonographer repositioned the probe and clicked some buttons, measuring the baby's size.

Xavier stared at the tiny baby on the screen. His feelings so big they were a painful mass expanding in his chest. But fear was dominant.

Then something miraculous happened. While

he and Lola watched, the baby moved, its tiny hand coming into focus. An eruption of love built inside him, a wave of indescribable emotion that left him certain he would, without doubt, protect and nurture that tiny human until the day he died. So this was parental love, a sickening tumult of joy and fear, and it had already begun.

'Are you okay?' Lola whispered, a serene smile on her face and her beautiful eyes awash with emotions.

He nodded, lost for words. How could she be so calm? What if she finally saw through him? Saw that he wasn't good enough to be a father? What if she one day rejected him and took his baby away?

'Did you see it move?' she asked. 'See the tiny fluttering heartbeat?'

He nodded again, leaning forward to press a breathless kiss to the back of Lola's hand, vowing there and then that if she let him, he would always care for her and the baby to the absolute best of his ability.

'Does everything look okay?' he croaked, addressing both Lola, who would have seen scans before through her work, and the sonographer.

Lola nodded and the sonographer confirmed it. 'The baby is growing well, the size consistent with the dates of your last period.' She printed off a couple of pictures and handed them over. 'Your due date is the sixth of January. Congratulations.'

Xavier stared at the picture, his heart in his throat and time speeding up. He had approximately seven months to prepare for the biggest life-change he was ever likely to encounter. Seven months to pull himself together, to figure out how best to share their child with Lola. Because now that he'd experienced that rush of parental love, he absolutely, categorically, could not mess this up.

CHAPTER THIRTEEN

XAVIER SILENTLY HELD onto Lola's hand for much of the rest of the appointment, which included a brief examination by the obstetrician to confirm that all was well with the pregnancy.

Her heart clenched for him. He was obviously going through some momentous feelings, not that he would share them with her of course. But as they left St Sebastian's side by side, Lola tugged his hand to bring him to a halt near her car, pushing to be let in.

'It's overwhelming, isn't it?' she said, identifying his bewildered expression, part of her feeling something similar. She cared about him the way he cared about her. She wanted them to share not just the highs of this pregnancy, but also any fears they might have. She needed him to be on the same wavelength, so they could support each other through the next seven months as well as through the birth and the newborn stage.

'I guess it is,' he said, seeming distracted and

withdrawn. Maybe he was already thinking about the princess and London.

Lola sighed, a strange flood of panic washing over her. Lying in his arms that morning, she'd been filled with excitement and optimism, but now that they held photographic evidence of their baby in their hands, she was suddenly besieged by doubts.

Maybe it had been a mistake to start sleeping with him again. Because since they'd surrendered to their passion, she couldn't seem to stop. Only in the back of her mind, she knew she must and soon. She couldn't afford to develop feelings for him. Not when she was still trying to figure out where she wanted her career to take her. Not when Xavier had no interest in a real relationship. Not when each of them had set aside the search for commitment for their own reasons, hers to prove that she could excel in her career and his because he'd needed to fill a hole in his life.

He held up the scan picture. 'I can't quite believe it. I know it's true, but it feels…surreal.'

'I know.' Lola glanced again at his picture. Hers was tucked safely in her bag. 'The first scan makes it way more real. That's our baby.'

Was he having doubts, too? Was he gearing up to end their fling and focus instead on them being parents?

'If I feel it's appropriate,' he said, 'do you mind if I tell the princess, about the baby?' He still clutched his copy of the sonogram picture as if it were precious.

'Of course not,' Lola said, the reality of Xavier's earlier warnings hitting home.

That tiny baby had some big shoes to fill—a historic estate, a lucrative business, a title and royal relations. Just like Lola had once protected herself from simply slotting into Nicolás's ready-made life, she would need to protect her child from the weight of such a responsibility. Every child deserved a carefree childhood. She and Xavier had both had one, and she would make certain that no matter what the future held for them as parents, their baby's happiness would come first.

'Are *you* okay,' he said, taking her hand once more, his stare searching hers so she felt close to tears suddenly.

'I'm fine,' she said. 'A bit emotional and overwhelmed. It's all finally hitting home. But sadly I need to head back to the clinic. And you have a plane to catch.'

She smiled, hiding her disappointment with the timing of his trip to London. She was secretly dreading being at Casa Colina without him, even for one night. She'd hoped they would talk about the baby this evening after they'd each had time to process the scan. She would miss him and couldn't help but draw parallels between Xavier's life and the life of duty she'd once rejected.

Xavier nodded, wrapped one arm around her neck, drawing her close and pressing a kiss to her forehead. 'I'm not telling you what to do, but please be careful. If you want, I can arrange for Carlos to pick you up from work tonight, so you don't have to face the paps alone.'

Of course he would worry about her safety. His thoughtfulness and the extra security team he'd employed were touching but practical. But it was too much to hope that he might actually miss her in return.

'Thanks, but I'll be fine.' Lola looked up at him with her brave face in place. She shouldn't want him to miss her. They weren't a couple. They'd only been living under the same roof for a matter of weeks. But they'd spent every spare moment together. They'd slept in the same bed, had sex in every one of the villa's rooms, including every single guest room. They'd eaten breakfast together, sometimes in bed, travelled to and from work together, swam and walked the estate together. Maybe she was simply emotional because of the baby.

'See you tomorrow then,' he said, looking as if he wanted to say more, but had stopped himself. Then he glanced down at her stomach. 'Both of you.'

Lola's heart leapt. Of course he was thinking about the baby. Lola knew he cared about her—he showed her that every day. But she needed to remember that his consideration was largely because she was carrying his child. It wasn't about *her*.

'Good luck with Princess Xiomara,' she said, before she could embarrass herself by welling up in hormonal tears. She rested her hand on his chest, over the reassuring thump of his heart. 'Just be yourself. Any family would be lucky to have you.'

She was certain that when the de la Rosa got to know him as a man not just and employee, they would see the loyal and compassionate man she saw. Except she doubted any of them, her included, would ever see his whole, vulnerable self.

'That's the only person I can be,' he said with confidence.

But deep down, she knew him well enough to understand that he most likely had doubts. After all, he'd once worked for the princess, keeping her safe. With his feelings for their mutual father so… resentful, he would likely struggle to feel comfortable that she was actually his half-sister.

Brushing her lips over his in a swift goodbye kiss, she said, 'Safe travels.'

She unlocked her car, desperate to get away before she blurted out something stupid, like how much she'd miss him or how she wished he'd let her in, or how, sometimes, when she was alone, she thought she might want more than sex. Praying that was simply her hormones talking, she started the engine.

Today was a wake-up call. She couldn't get used to having him around. Them living together was a temporary measure and nothing to do with feelings. Xavier didn't do serious relationships and the last time she'd trusted her instincts when it came to love, she'd almost married a man who hadn't loved her in return. Who'd only wanted her to complete some family portrait he could hang on the wall of his ancient estate alongside his ancestors.

She'd always wanted more than an empty relationship that looked good on the surface. If she wasn't careful with Xavier, who no matter what they'd shared always seemed to be holding himself back, she'd get hurt.

As she drove away, she couldn't resist one last glance at him through the rear-view mirror, a view she should perhaps, get used to.

It was gone midnight, officially the next day when Xavier finally returned home to Casa Colina. After his meeting with the princess, or Xiomara as she'd insisted he call her from now on, the idea of spending the night in a faceless London hotel, miles away from Lola, left him cold. Especially today, when together they'd finally seen their baby. So, instead of tossing and turning through a fitful night's sleep in a strange bed where he knew his doubts would plague him, he'd jumped on the last flight leaving London for Castilona.

Quietly climbing the stairs after touching base with Carlos and Marco, he already felt better just knowing they were back under the same roof. He paused outside his room and glanced down the hallway. There was a light coming from Lola's bedroom. The door was ajar.

Unable to resist checking on her, he peeked inside, his heart galloping at the sight of her asleep, an open book still clutched in her hand. He swallowed the lump in his throat, watching her breathe for a few minutes, glad that he'd gone with his instincts and returned tonight. This beautiful, intelligent woman had turned his world upside down with her news. She'd given him a wondrous gift in his child, given him the sense of belonging he'd always craved.

But now came the tricky part. He needed to treat her with care. His current physical addiction to her would soon fade and then they would have bigger issues to discuss than whether to sleep in his bed or hers.

Silently, he crept into the room and carefully removed the book from her hand, placing it on the nightstand. He was about to turn off the lamp when Lola stirred.

'Xavier...?'

'Sorry,' he whispered. 'I didn't mean to wake you. You fell asleep with the lamp on.'

She sat up, rested on her elbow and reached for his hand. 'You came home early.'

Home? He couldn't bear to tell her that this stunning villa didn't feel like home, or at least it hadn't until she'd moved in. She'd brought laughter there. Lit up the rooms with her smile. And most of all, she'd given him a reason to preserve the traditions of this place for their child. That was the one easy thing he could do as a father.

'Is everything okay?' she asked sleepily. 'How did it go with the princess?'

Xavier allowed her to pull him down to the bed and sat on the edge beside her, his hand far too comfortable in hers. But then every time they touched it gave him a buzz and left him hungry for more. What the hell was happening to him? And how could he make it stop before it got any worse? Before he let her all the way in and she saw the real him? Before she found something lacking?

Fearing it might already be too late, he focussed on his visit with the princess. 'It was fine. A bit awkward at first. She kept insisting that I drop the "princess" and simply call her Xiomara, correcting me every time I used her title.' Which was every time he'd addressed her.

'Yes, you would struggle with that,' Lola said with an indulgent smile. As if she knew him better than anyone. 'It took you seven months to call me Lola.'

'Old habits die hard, I guess,' he said, his thumb stroking the back of her hand, which was warm and soft and distracted him from the idea that he was balanced on the top of a precariously stacked pile of furniture. One wrong move and everything would come tumbling down.

'It's understandable given you protected her for so many years,' Lola went on. 'But don't forget that she's also just a person, irrespective of any title.'

Xavier fell quiet, Lola's insight hitting right at the heart of his doubts. He suspected he'd never feel comfortable around the royal family now that he no longer worked for them. Not because they were cold or superior, but because he would always feel like an imposter in their world. In his own life, the small but secure safety net he'd built around himself, he knew exactly who he was. His needs were few and simple. Those he could trust and rely upon even fewer.

'I know it's not easy for you to embrace your new family,' she said, clinging to his hand. 'But if you let them see the real you, I'm sure they'll come to value and respect you for the man you are.'

'*I* know who I am,' he said, his pulse buzzing in his ears. 'That's all that matters. I don't need acceptance from the de la Rosas. And any relationship we might have in the future will always be complicated by the past.'

'I know,' she agreed, looking hurt by his dismissal. 'But just like you deserve to know them as family, they deserve to know you, too. I know it's scary to let people in,' she said, her touch soothing the torture of her words. 'Especially after what you've been through. But you're someone worth knowing, Xavier.'

Xavier stayed silent, wishing he'd kissed her when she'd awoken so that they might be naked by now instead of dissecting his damaged psyche—his least favourite pastime.

'Does anyone know the real you?' he asked, his pulse leaping at how close she was to tearing away his final shield. His final layer of protection. 'You once said we all have uncomfortable secrets.'

She looked down at their clasped hands then met his stare once more. 'You're right. I've been scared too in the past. Not of letting someone close but of trusting myself to know when a relationship is right. Ever since I ended my engagement, I've been trying to prove to myself that I made the right choice in choosing my career over my personal life. I've been scared to make a mistake and find myself trapped in a life that isn't mine. But that means I've been denying a whole part of my life that needs attention. I don't want to be alone for ever. One day, I want it all. My career, a family, love.'

His mouth dried, jealousy for the future man whom Lola would one day love turning his stomach. 'How will you know when you've found it? This relationship that's right?' He'd always assumed seeking out commitment was too risky, but lately the idea of losing what he and Lola had seemed even more terrifying.

But he couldn't selfishly hold onto her. She deserved to be loved, to find happiness, to have it all. Of course, that would also mean some other man would be raising his child...

'I'll know, because I'll want to give it my all,' she said, making it sound so simple, highlighting their differences.

'Then I hope you find what you're looking for,' he said, knowing *he* couldn't make her any promises.

'I hope you do, too,' she said sadly, as if she pitied him. And maybe she did. Because she'd always seen him far too clearly.

Needing to show her that he would be okay without her, without the kind of love he'd never experienced and feared he was incapable of, he said, 'I think, after today, after meeting our baby, I've already found where I belong—it's fatherhood.' He met her stare, his chest tight, his emotions so close to the surface. 'A part of me was scared that I'd be like him, be a terrible father.'

Lola frowned and shook her head.

'But after today...when I saw the baby move... I don't know, something happened. I vowed that I would die trying to be the kind of father our baby deserves.' The kind that every baby deserved.

'Xavier...' Lola whispered, her eyes shining with tears. 'You're going to be amazing.'

'Don't cry,' he said, cupping her face, the ache for her he'd carried with him to London intensifying. 'I'll let you get some rest. It's late. We can talk tomorrow.' He stood, leaned over her to kiss her, but she grabbed his hand.

'Don't go. I want you to stay.' She peeled back the covers invitingly.

Xavier hesitated, that self-protective core of his battling with his desire to hold her, to sleep with her and his baby in his arms, to drift off praying that everything would work out.

The decision made, Xavier heeled off his shoes, simultaneously removing his shirt, his jeans and socks following. Wearing only his boxers, he climbed in alongside her. The bed was warm with her body heat, the linens scented with her perfume. Her silky slip-clad body fitting into his arms until their hearts rested side by side, her back to his front.

She snuggled, entwining her legs with his, her arms around his arms, which held her close. 'The house was too quiet without you,' she whispered.

'It was like that before you came to stay,' he said, pressing a kiss to her neck, breathing in the warm scent of her skin so the panicked feeling enslaving him all day, eased. 'It's just too big for one person.'

She sighed. 'I guess it won't be quiet for long, not with a baby around.'

'That's fine with me,' he said, sensing her smile, needing her promises that they would share the baby, no matter what. Because the longer they delayed the conversation they needed to have, the more space there seemed for doubts.

Telling himself that he trusted Lola, he finally allowed himself to drift off to sleep.

CHAPTER FOURTEEN

THE NEXT MORNING, as they travelled the coastal road to the clinic for what would be one of their final days working together, Xavier asked Lola a question that had been spinning in his mind for weeks.

'I wondered if you'd come to Princess Xiomara's wedding this weekend as my plus one?' he asked. 'Not a date just... Well, apparently, it's not the done thing to fly solo and you know how I hate making small talk.'

From the passenger seat, Lola glanced his way, her expression guarded. 'Won't us being seen together create gossip, even if it's not a date?'

By laying low at Casa Colina and using Xavier's vehicles with tinted windows, they'd managed to avoid being photographed together. Xavier's hands tightened on the wheel, disappointment leaving a sour taste in his mouth. Her voice was strange. Tense. As if their talk late last night had upset her—the last thing he wanted to do. And he had no clue how to fix it. But they weren't a couple. Having spent his entire adult life avoiding close connections, he had no idea how to be that vulnerable with someone. No matter how much he might want to try.

'The reception will be held at the palace,' he said. 'Press are strictly forbidden. I only care that you'll be safe, which I'm confident you will there otherwise I'd never have suggested it. But I understand if you'd prefer not to come.'

'Okay,' she said quietly, thoughtfully. 'Can I think about it and let you know?'

'Of course,' he said, this relationship with Lola pushing him way out of his comfort zone. Lola had gently pushed and pushed since the night of the storm, exposing his feelings as if he had an endless supply to give, as if she wanted more of him than he was perhaps capable of giving. As if his best wasn't good enough or maybe that was unfair and simply his own doubts talking.

Just as they rounded a tight bend in the road, they came across a cloud of dust and a motorbike lying on the verge.

'Pull over,' Lola said, at the same moment Xavier flicked on his indicator.

'Someone's had an accident,' he said as he parked safely, leaving his hazard lights on to warn any other vehicles.

Together they hurried towards the bike, which was unattended. Xavier pulled his phone from his pocket to call the police. Lola inched towards the edge of the cliff and carefully peered over.

'There's a casualty down there,' she said, gripping Xavier's arm. 'He looks unconscious. I'm going down to him.'

'We should wait for help.' Xavier grabbed her hand, the metallic taste of fear on his tongue. 'You can't go down there. It's dangerous.'

A moment's determination flashed in her eyes. 'He needs help now. I'll be fine,' she argued, tugging her arm free and gingerly beginning to scramble down the slope, which was covered in scrub. No discernible path obvious.

'Be careful. Wait for me,' he yelled just before the call to emergency services connected. He quickly informed the emergency dispatcher of the location of the accident. Then he hung up and followed after Lola, clutching at handfuls of grass and bracken and sliding down the slope on his backside to get to her quickly.

His fingers curled around her upper arm, relief choking him. 'You could fall too,' he said, pleading. 'Think about the baby.'

He wasn't telling her how to behave, but nor did he want to see her throw herself headlong into a dangerous situation.

'Then help me,' she cried, proceeding despite his warning, although she kept a hold of his hand so they could slowly and carefully descend together.

With one hand on Lola, Xavier clung to the vegetation as they slipped and scrabbled towards the man. He was lying lifeless on a small ledge, held in place by the trunk of a tree without which, he would have surely fallen to the rocks and ocean below.

When they finally reached the casualty, Lola felt for a pulse and listened for breath sounds.

'He's alive,' she said, opening his leather motorbike jacket to search for other injuries.

Xavier noticed the unnatural angle of his foot. 'He's got a broken leg by the looks of it,' he told her, also scanning for injuries, although the man's crash helmet prevented them from assessing his head.

When Lola's hand came out of the man's jacket covered in blood, their fears intensified.

'I think he has a penetrating chest wound,' she said, glancing up at the road as the sound of distant sirens reached them.

'There's not much we can do beyond maintain his airway,' Xavier reasoned. They had no equipment, they were perched on the edge of a steep drop and the ambulance was on its way.

'I'm not leaving him,' she said, bracing her hand on the trunk of the tree as she shifted closer. She wobbled, righting herself quickly, but Xavier's pulse exploded as he envisioned her at the bottom of the cliff.

Because of his vision issues, the bottom of the

cliff was a blurry abyss. He had no concept of how far the drop actually was, but his fears for Lola and the baby intensified, a tight band of pressure around his temples.

'I'm staying too,' he said. 'Please be careful. Just stay there. Don't move. Help is on its way.'

Within tense, fear-filled minutes, the police, ambulance and fire service arrived. A fire officer and paramedic secured by ropes and safety harnesses descended the slope to join them and assess the situation up close.

'I think he's impaled on a branch,' Lola told them.

The fire officer radioed for a saw to be lowered. With the branch cut from the tree they set about securing the unconscious man to the stretcher that had also been lowered. Slowly, they hauled him up the slope inch by inch to the waiting ambulance, the paramedic following.

'Let's get you two safely up to the road,' the fire officer said. 'We don't want another accident.'

'Her first,' Xavier told him, reaching for the safety harness the team above lowered and helping Lola into it. 'She's pregnant,' he told the other man, who nodded reassuringly.

Lola shot Xavier an annoyed look he ignored. Until he had her safe on firm ground away from the cliff, he wouldn't rest.

The fire crew hoisted Lola up the slope, followed by Xavier, the rescue complete. By the time he'd made it to the road, Lola was in the back of the ambulance, updating the paramedics.

Xavier's insides trembled with adrenaline. He wanted to drag Lola close and ensure she was unharmed. He...cared about her. How could he not? She was having his baby, living in his house, sleeping in his bed. He'd begun to wonder if, for Lola, he might break the habit of a lifetime and give a committed relationship a shot rather than lose her. But even if he could change and let her into his life, would she want him? She wanted it all. She wanted and deserved love. He wouldn't be enough for her and he might ruin what they already had—respect, a connection through their child and commitment as parents.

Panicked, he dragged in some deep calming breaths, fearing it was impossible to be objective around Lola. His feelings were brittle. His protective urges in overdrive, leaving him irrational and helpless. He'd already let her close and now she had the power to destroy him. To rip his safe world to pieces. He watched her climb down from the back of the ambulance more unsettled and confused than ever before.

Lola stepped from the back of the ambulance wiping some of the blood from her hands with wet wipes the paramedics had given her. Xavier stood stiffly waiting, his face set in an angry scowl she ignored. Together, they watched the ambulance pull away, an awful tension building between them.

After briefly giving their names and address to the police, they headed back to the car in stony silence. Late last night, when he'd shared his fears for fatherhood with her, she'd felt as if she was finally making a breakthrough with him. That he was finally letting her close. She'd fallen asleep in his arms, nursing the first flicker of hope that maybe, just maybe, they might be able to build on what they had and have a real relationship. But now, in the cold light of day and with anger and resentment simmering just beneath the surface, she simply felt stupid.

I wondered if you'd come to Princess Xiomara's wedding this weekend as my plus one? Not a date...

His words from earlier rang through her head, mocking how much more invested in this relationship she was compared to him. But then Xavier had always protected himself. Holding back from her, from everyone, to keep himself safe from rejection.

'I'll take you home,' he said, unlocking the vehicle and opening her door.

'I'm fine. I need to go to work.' She cast him a determined look and climbed into the passenger seat, in no mood for his mollycoddling.

'You're covered in blood, Lola,' he pointed out as if she wasn't aware.

'It wouldn't be the first time,' she said. 'And I have a change of clothes at my office.' She pulled on her seatbelt. 'I'll clean up there.'

Xavier pressed his lips together and started the engine, pulling out onto the road, disapproval seeping from him.

'You're annoyed with me,' she said after a few minutes of unbearable silence.

'I'm concerned for you,' he said in that infuriatingly calm voice. 'I know you're a doctor and you need to help people, but you won't be able to do that if you're dead at the bottom of a cliff.'

'I was safe,' she argued. 'I'm not stupid.' Apart from with her feelings, which despite her best attempts, craved more and more and more of him. Whereas he was still safely emotionally contained.

'You're pregnant,' he retaliated.

'Yes, I'm pregnant, not incapacitated.' She tried and failed to keep the mocking tone from her voice. 'It's not the Victorian era, Xavier. Pregnant women don't need to be confined to bed rest these days.'

Why were they having their first fight? Was it because with every day she woke up in his arms, every time they reached for each other making passionate love as if the end was coming, she saw things more clearly. She *was* at risk. At risk of falling for him. Whereas he seemed to only care about the baby. Not about her.

But then he'd warned her he was uninterested in anything beyond sex. If she'd imagined that his touch, his kisses, the way he held her was more than that, she only had herself to blame.

'You scared me,' he said quietly, his eyes on the road.

'I'm sorry.' Compassion welled up inside her. They were both making this up as they went along and Xavier was safety obsessed. 'That wasn't my intention. I would never have put myself in a situation I felt was dangerous.'

'So you're not planning to take our baby overseas to some war-torn country or humanitarian crisis then?'

'Of course not,' she reasoned. 'That was the plan before I discovered I was pregnant. You're just lashing out now.'

She understood he might be reeling. Coming to terms with the fact he was going to be a father when he'd never known his own father and had some pretty major hang ups about his ability to adopt the role, but if he'd only let her in, they could discuss his fears in a rational way.

'I'm not lashing out, Lola, I'm scared. I have no idea what your plans are for the rest of the pregnancy or for after the birth. For all I know you're moving back to Spain, where you'll strap the baby into a baby carrier and carry it around the hospital while you do your job. I've tried to give you space and time, but we need to discuss all of this, Lola. It's my baby too.'

'I hope you're not suggesting that I can no longer work,' she scoffed, 'just because I've had a baby.' It was as if he didn't understand her at all. As if he hadn't heard a thing she'd told him about Nicolás and the past and her need to be independent.

'Of course I'm not saying that,' he said shooting her a look of hurt and confusion. 'I would never say such a thing. You're free to do whatever you like. You're free to move out of Casa Colina. Free to take any job you want anywhere in the world. I told you I'd move with you. I'm not trying to clip your wings. I just want you to be safe. I need to know the baby is safe and I need to be a part of its life.'

'I know that.' Lola deflated, the fight draining out of her as he pulled into the underground car park at the clinic. How could she argue with his reasonable logic? Of course they weren't a couple. And he was right. She'd been putting off finalising her plans because she'd been struggling to imagine what her life would become. But she could see now how her indecision might have made Xavier feel off-balance.

'Look…' She sighed, turning to face him as he parked the car. 'I know you need answers and I wish I had them for you, but I guess a part of me, a part I hadn't even realised existed until we went for the scan, has been in denial that my life is about to change.'

He reached for her hand and Lola clung to his fingers, regret a weight on her shoulders.

'I've been restless for a while,' she said, glancing at her lap, fighting her inclination to interpret how wonderful he was as a sign that he might have feelings for *her*. 'I thought I needed a change of medical scenery. But... I don't know. Maybe I just need to step off the professional treadmill I've been on since nineteen and really examine what it is I want to do with the rest of my career. I've thought about doing a master's degree, but I'm also dealing with the fact that the baby will also bring changes.'

'We're both dealing with that,' he said softly.

She nodded, her tangle of feelings suddenly close to the surface. For days now, every time they laughed together or when they made love, the force of their passion and their connection had overwhelmed her and she realised how easily she could develop deep feelings for this man. Not just because he was the father of their baby, but because he made her feel secure. That she could always be herself because he was always himself. That he was solid and dependable and would always be there if she or their child needed him.

But of course he couldn't be the right man for her. He didn't want to be the right man. He believed himself incapable of romantic love. But he had so much more to give. Maybe somewhere along the way, while pushing and trying to get to know him, she'd lost sight of *his* needs.

'I know you're a protector,' she said. 'You need to know that those around you are safe, so I want to reassure you. I'm fully committed to us raising this baby together. I'm not going anywhere without a discussion with you first. I promise.'

Although how she would watch him be the wonderful father she knew he was capable of being and not want him still, want all of him, was enough to make her wonder if she should end their physical relationship now, before she slipped any further under his spell. Her apartment was still leased for a few more days. Maybe she should put some distance between them and move back there.

'I only want to keep those around me safe because...' He swallowed, obviously struggling to explain. 'As wonderful a mother as Carlota was,' he said, 'never knowing my father made me feel...untethered. He could have been any man I saw walking down the street. I was free to imagine every possible scenario, from the fact that he might have forced himself on my mother to the fact that he had another family somewhere and I had a sibling, which, as it happens, turned out to be true.'

She cupped his face, held his stare to hers, aware he was trying his best to be more open.

'I'm sorry. Of course you wanted your world to have boundaries, to feel secure, to make sense of something that...' she shook her head, choked, '...seems inexplicable to me.' How any parent with means could disown their own child was unfathomable. 'But he didn't deserve you, Xavier. You're a strong and honourable man. A natural leader with a huge heart. *He* was unworthy of *you*.'

His expression tortured, he pulled her into his arms, buried his face against her neck. She held him, both euphoric that he'd let her in and heartbroken that he'd spent so much of his life lost, trying to make sense of a senseless situation. Her heart clenched for him. He wanted to be a good father, to be nothing like his own. He would always love their child and that would need to be enough for Lola.

Easing away, she popped her seatbelt and forced herself to take an emotional step back. 'Of course, I can't live with you for ever. I'll find my own place again, soon. I might at some point want to go back to Spain. I might one day meet someone and want a serious relationship.' She bravely met his stare, catching sight of the same flicker of fear she'd seen last night when they'd talked about her wanting it all. But his fear was for his relationship with the baby, not for *her*. 'But I promise you we'll always figure out what's best for our baby together, okay?'

They stared at each other for a few moments.

Lola emulated him, closing down that part of her that had begun to harbour hope and foolish fantasies. Where she, Xavier and the baby were a real family. But the last thing she wanted was a gloss-covered relationship like the one Nicolás had been offering. If she ever fell in love again, she wanted the grit and fire and chaos of a love that was fearless, bold and mindlessly passionate.

'I'd better go,' she said, placing her hand on the door handle, scared at how close she'd come to falling for him.

'Wait…' he said, resting his hand on her knee. 'I'm sorry, I overreacted earlier. I have no right to tell you what to do.'

Lola nodded, a part of her wishing he'd fight for her, the way she wanted to fight for him. Hungry for all of him. The parts he gave readily, like his loyalty and his protection and his passion, and the parts he held back, like his fears and his dreams and the very heart of him.

But maybe he was truly incapable of letting someone that close. Maybe he was already giving all that he could give and she was just a fool to expect more the way she'd almost made a terrible mistake before. She needed to stop pushing, to protect herself and adjust her expectations, otherwise, she *would* get hurt.

'See you tonight,' she said, leaving the car, the clack of her heels across the concrete of the car park echoing like a bad omen.

CHAPTER FIFTEEN

That weekend, after a lavish state ceremony joining Princess Xiomara de la Rosa to Dr Edmund Butler, Xavier stood stiffly in the great hall of the palace, where everything glittered and sparkled in celebration of another joyous royal wedding. All around him, people wore smiles as they mingled and chatted and sipped champagne. The newlyweds circulated, speaking to their guests, but Xavier could barely drag his eyes away from Lola.

She looked stunningly beautiful in a royal blue dress, her hair artfully pinned up to reveal the elegant slope of her neck. But she also looked nervous and a little tired. Royal weddings were an all-day event and they were less than half way through this one.

Foreign urges swamped him. He wanted to hold her, to proudly introduce her to the princess, to say something—anything—to stop her slipping through his fingers. Because he felt it.

'I think they're heading this way,' Lola said,

stiffening slightly at his side as she glanced at the beaming bride and groom.

Without thinking, he rested his hand in the small of her back and dipped his head to whisper, 'You've met before. Just be yourself.'

'Don't,' she said quietly, stepping out of his reach so his hand fell away. 'I don't want to fuel any gossip.'

Her stare was imploring, but Xavier winced, his heart thudding painfully, terrifyingly, as it had since the day after he'd returned from London. Something had changed. Lola seemed to be putting more and more distance between them. Her disappointment seemed to taint every gentle word she spoke to him. Her withdrawal ruined every touch and kiss. And he had no right to expect anything else. They weren't a couple. The only promise he'd made her was one of protection. He could try and hold onto her, to give her more, but what if his attempts to let her in and be what she needed still weren't enough? She deserved love. The all-consuming, unconditional, mindless kind.

'We only met briefly,' she said about the princess, her eyes on the couple. Her expression softened. 'She looks so beautiful. And happy.'

Xavier swallowed at the wistfulness in Lola's voice and the resulting spike in his panicked heart rate. Last night, they'd finally had their long overdue talk about the future. Lola had agreed to stay in Castilona until the baby was born. Xavier reiterated that, if she favoured returning to Spain for work or study after her maternity leave, he would relocate there at that point, leaving the estate under its current management.

Their civilised and reasonable talk should have reassured him, but all he'd felt since was growing dread. Fear of losing her jostled with the fear of trying and failing to be the man she deserved. Those fears hounding him no matter how often he made love to her, worshipping her body, pleasuring her into incoherence as if he could fix what he'd broken so she would once more look at him the way she had before everything began to go wrong.

'Xavier,' Princess Xiomara said, holding out her hands as she walked towards him, elegantly trailing her dress and the floor-length veil she wore. Taking his hands, she pulled him close, pressing her cheek to each of his.

When she released him, Xavier bowed at the waist, his sense of duty battling with the need to be alone with Lola. 'Princess, you look breathtaking.'

Xiomara frowned slightly at his use of her title, but she seemed far too happy to be cross with him.

'Congratulations,' he said to them both, shaking Edmund's hand. 'You remember Dr Lola Garcia from *Clinico San Carlos*.'

'Of course,' the princess said warmly, greeting Lola with the same cheek kisses. 'May I present my husband, Dr Edmund Butler, whom of course you've both met before. He wasn't my husband then, but he is now and I like saying it.' She smiled playfully at the man at her side.

'What a beautiful ceremony,' Lola said, her eyes shining with sincerity. 'I hope you'll both be very happy.'

'Thank you,' the princess said as Butler asked Xavier about the medals he wore on his uniform before engaging Lola in talk of the clinic and the new medical director.

'She looks tired,' Xiomara said in a low voice about Lola.

Xavier nodded. 'She's been a little nauseous these past few days.' Guilt added to his other emotions.

'I asked the palace housekeepers to prepare a room for your use, just in case you needed a moment to yourselves,' Xiomara said. 'Perhaps you could take Lola there before the banquet begins so she might have a lie down. These state occasions can feel dreadfully long when you're not the centre of attention.'

She smiled, but because he'd known her so long, he saw the flicker of concern in her eyes.

'Thank you. I'll suggest it to Lola.' A reprieve from the small talk and a moment to themselves might help.

'I know you're not together,' she said, carefully,

'but I must say, you make a very attractive couple. I'm sure that when he or she arrives, my baby nephew or niece will be utterly adorable.' She squeezed Xavier's arm. 'I can't wait.'

Xavier tried to smile, to let her know he appreciated her attempts to make him feel part of the family, but all he could do was nod, his gaze returning to Lola. How would things be between them by the time the baby arrived? Could they find a way to be together? Could he offer her more of a commitment and hope it was enough? The alternative, to let her go, for them to just be friends and parents felt equally terrifying.

'We'll talk later,' Xiomara told him before scooping her arm through her husband's before leading him away to greet more of their guests.

'You have the same eyes,' Lola said when they were once more alone. 'It's obvious now that you two are related.' She looked up at him, the ghost of a sad smile on her lips.

'Is it?' he said, not yet comfortable with such comparisons, which only reminded him of de la Rosa, a man to whom he never wanted to be compared, least of all by Lola. 'We're very different personalities. The princess has always been unapologetically herself, something I've always admired.'

'Yes.' Lola nodded, looking at him appraisingly. 'I'm glad that she found a way to break free of her father's influence. She seems nothing like the man I've heard rumours about.'

Xavier stilled, his heart thudding. He too, of course, was related to the man at the centre of those rumours. Were his past attempts to protect himself, the way he habitually shut people out, Lola included, turning into his worst character flaw? Was Lola now having doubts that he could be a good father to their baby?

'She's had a room prepared, if you'd like to lie down for a while,' he said, his own doubts building at the strange tension between them because he had no idea how to make things right.

Lola nodded. 'That sounds wonderful actually. I should have reconsidered the height of these heels. My feet are killing me.'

'Let's slip away,' he said keeping his hands to himself when every instinct in him wanted to touch her. But that was selfish. She didn't want his touch and didn't belong to him, no matter how badly he wanted her. He'd always respected that she was her own woman. 'Let's find a steward and locate the room,' he said, hoping that after a rest, Lola might seem more herself and he might find the right words to make her stay.

After a nap and a shower in the most lavish bathroom she'd ever experienced, Lola tied the belt of her robe and faced herself in the mirror.

The royal wedding had been everything it

should be—traditional, uplifting, romantic. The palace was the most breathtaking venue for a ceremony, every meticulous detail perfection. And Lola should never have agreed to come. Looking down she breathed through the growing hollowness in her chest.

Having witnessed the joy and intimacy of other people's love today, not just the princess and Edmund, but also the King and Queen, who'd proudly each held one of their adorable twins, Lola had finally found the strength to admit to herself that she too had fallen in love. With Xavier.

Dropping her hand to her stomach, she blinked away the tears threatening to fall. She had to be strong for the baby. For herself. And she had to move out of Casa Colina. Tonight. As soon as they left the celebrations. She would move back to her apartment. Find another to rent. Maybe visit her family in Spain and return here strengthened. Ready to face him and pretend.

Opening the bathroom door, she stepped into the bedroom to find Xavier sitting at the window, the room dimly lit with lamplight. The suite prepared for them was on the ground floor, with French doors that opened to the rear gardens. A light breeze made the drapes billow and carried the scent of flowers from outside where the distant lights of coastal towns snaked out of sight around the headland.

'Feeling better?' he asked, holding out his hand for hers, then tugging her into his lap.

'Yes,' she said, the lie coming easily, because to tell the truth would be to ruin, once and for all what they had, not that any of it had been real anyway. She'd simply convinced herself that her heart was safe when the reality was she'd fallen harder than she'd ever before been in love.

Curling into his lap, she buried her face against his neck, wishing she had the strength to leave him now. But he had a formal banquet to get through, followed by dancing and an entire evening of small talk.

Forcing herself to make memories for the tough times ahead when she would miss him as if a part of her soul was lost, she breathed in the scent of his skin, closing her eyes so she could cling to the illusion that he was hers for just a while longer.

'You looked so beautiful today,' he said, his hand stroking her back as she kissed his neck, trailed her tongue up to his earlobe, slipped her hand inside his open dress shirt where his skin burned hot and his heart thudded against her palm.

'Lola…?' he said, growing hard under her lap.

She looked up and saw desire in his dark eyes, but confusion too, as if he had no idea how to interpret her strange mood. But this time, she couldn't help him. Her strength was just enough to make it through the rest of the day in his company and then leave.

'I want you,' she said, capturing his lips, kissing him, darting out her tongue to meet his when he opened his mouth. She wanted him, as always, but she also wanted more. She wanted him to love her as deeply as she loved him. She wanted the two of them to have it all—this connection she hadn't been able to fight, a family of their own and endless, passionate love.

Scared that those three little words might escape her lips, ruining the last few hours they had left together, she reached for the belt of his trousers. If this was the only part of him she could have, the only part of him she'd ever had, she would take it. Anything to delay, for a little longer, the inevitable end.

He groaned under her kisses. One arm around her waist, he slid his other hand along her leg and up her thigh under her robe. She tangled her fingers in his hair, kissing him harder as he delved between her legs where she was bare. Where she ached.

'Xavier,' she gasped as she stroked her. Then she twisted on his lap, sat astride his thighs, her back to the window and loosened the belt of her robe.

The fabric parted and his stare darkened as he took in her nakedness, his eyes devouring her the way they always had, as if he couldn't stop himself from touching. He cupped both her breasts, his thumbs rubbing her nipples into peaks. She moaned, thrust her chest forwards where he captured one nipple in his mouth and sucked.

'I need you,' she said, attacking his fly in earnest. He raised his hips and together they shoved down his trousers and underwear. Lola gripped him in her hand, tugging, stroking until his hands gripped her hips and he crushed her closer, as lost as she to this fire they generated.

She raised herself onto her knees then slowly sank onto him, tossing her head back as he filled her making her feel whole because she loved him. 'Xavier...'

His head was bent, his tongue lashing her nipple once more. She clung to his shoulders, rocking her hips, trying to ease the burning need inside. He held her hips, thrusting up into her so every stroke hit where she needed. All the reasons she must walk away from him, from this, fled her mind. Replaced by only pleasure, rightness and a longing that this could last for ever if only he'd open his heart to her.

She clung to his shoulders, crying out into the night as her orgasm struck. But still she couldn't let go, her arms banding around him as she rode wave after wave of spasms, as he stiffened, holding her just as tight and groaned his climax against her chest, their hearts thundering side by side.

'I love you,' she whispered into his hair, the

words slipping out during an unguarded moment of euphoria.

He froze. His ragged breathing the only movement he made. His silence the ultimate withdrawal.

Realising her mistake, Lola untangled herself from him and stood, tying the robe closed over her nakedness.

'I'm sorry,' she said, bitterly. 'I know that's the last thing you probably want to hear...' How could she have been so stupid?

Xavier stood and zipped up his fly. His appearance dishevelled. His stare haunted. 'I...' He speared a hand through his hair and turned away from her as if he couldn't bear the way she was looking at him.

'I can't hide it any more,' she said refusing to diminish her feelings. 'I shouldn't have to hide it. I don't want to. I love you, Xavier, like I've never loved anyone else.'

He stood stiffly, silently, his back to her.

'I know it wasn't part of the plan,' she said. 'But I just realised it today, at the wedding. The bride and groom are so in love. I looked over at you during the ceremony and it hit me.'

He paced behind the chair they'd just vacated then paced back. 'What do you want me to do... to say?' he asked, looking lost like a scared child. He really had no idea.

Lola crossed her arms over her waist. 'Nothing.

I guess I just hoped that you might have feelings for me in return. But I can see from your face that you don't.'

He gripped her arms, forced her to meet his stare. 'I *do* have feelings for you. I've never felt this way about anyone. Ever. I care about you. I want you to be happy. I want to protect you—'

'But you don't love me,' she said flatly. 'Not the way I love you.' She stood taller, stiffening her spine and her resolve to leave. Now. Before the pain worsened and destroyed her.

'Lola…'

'It's okay.' She shook her head, scared to hear what he had to say or wouldn't say. 'You don't have to make any excuses. But I need to leave Casa Colina. Tonight. I can't stay any longer.'

He dropped his hands, his handsome face slack with shock. 'No. It's late. Let's get through the banquet, go home and sleep on it. Talk about this in the morning.'

Lola marched to the bed where she'd left her change of clothes in her overnight bag. 'I can't. I need space.'

She pulled on clean underwear, threw on the dress she'd worn for the ceremony and reception and tossed the robe inside the bag, desperate to get away.

'You're leaving now? Leaving the wedding?'

'I'm sorry. I have to go. You'll be fine without me.' She hunted down her shoes and slid her feet inside. If she didn't get away from him soon, she was going to cry and beg him to love her.

'Lola… This is crazy. Wait.'

'It *is* crazy,' she said, all her frustration and heartache spilling free. 'I'm crazily in love with you. I want to fight for you and spend the rest of my life with you and raise a family with you and you have no idea what I'm feeling because you've kept your emotions under lock down and kept me out.'

'That's not true,' he said reaching for her again, his arms falling to his sides when she stepped back. 'I let you in. I've never let anyone else know me the way you do. I've told you things… We're having a baby. We agreed to raise it together. To make this work and now you're just walking out?'

'I'm sorry,' she said, tears finally falling. 'I want more.'

'Your independence?' he asked frowning.

She laughed hollowly, desolate that he had no idea how she felt. 'No. More of you, Xavier.'

'I…' His stare grew stormy. 'I gave you everything Lola. You pushed and kept on pushing and I gave you as much as I could. I told you about my fears of fatherhood. I shared my past with you, things I've never shared with anyone.'

'I know you tried. I know it's all you're capable of giving me and I wish it was enough. It would be so much easier, hurt so much less, if it were enough. I'm not blaming you.'

'But it's not enough?' he said, his voice dead.

'No.' She forced herself to be strong. 'I want it all. I wanted it all with you, but now I see that's not possible. That I've just made another mistake.'

'I… I don't know what more I can do.'

His words slashed her like knives. 'You can let me go. You can give me a few days to sort myself out. I need space.'

'But the baby…' he pleaded, his stare falling to her stomach.

'It's not about the baby. I promised we would raise the baby together and we will. But I can't stay loving you and knowing that you only want me around because I'm carrying your child.'

'That's not true. I…'

Unable to stay a second longer, she scooped up her bag. 'I'll be at my apartment. Please, if you care about me as you say you do, give me a few days. Then we'll talk.'

Without a backward glance, she fled.

CHAPTER SIXTEEN

TWO DAYS LATER, the crackle of static from the walkie talkie on his desk snapped Xavier out of the trance he'd existed in since Lola had left him that night of the royal wedding. He snatched it up, his heart rate spiking with adrenaline and hope. Had she changed her mind and come back to Casa Colina? Had she decided that he was enough for her after all?

'Princess Xiomara is on her way,' Marco's voice said through the walkie talkie.

Xavier's stomach fell. Hope a wisp of smoke, gone in a second. Of course Lola wouldn't have come back to him. She'd told him that she loved him and he'd let her go, scared to open his mouth and explain everything he was feeling. Flailing because she deserved it all, everything she wanted, and he knew nothing about romantic love.

'Thank you,' Xavier replied, too bereft to wonder why the princess was there when she must be about to leave for her honeymoon.

Dragging himself to his feet, he ran a hand over

his face and the two days' worth of scruff, wondering just how haggard he appeared and if Xiomara would notice. With Lola gone and Xavier once more alone at Casa Colina, time had lost its meaning. The estate work waiting for his attention went undone. Tired of throwing his untouched meals in the bin, Tia had stopped cooking for him. And sleep…forget it. He spent all night staring at the walls of his study, his mind a confusing swirl of regret, frustration and fear.

Just as he made it to the hall, Princess Xiomara arrived, a flurry of energy and floaty fabric, waving off her security guard as she breezed Xavier's way, arms outstretched.

'I came to thank you for everything you did at the wedding,' she said, embracing him with a double cheek kiss.

Xavier stiffened, too bereft to conceal his reaction to being hugged. Too confused to do more than stand and stare.

'Shouldn't you be with your new husband?' he asked at last.

'We're leaving soon, for our honeymoon…' the princess said, '…but I wanted to say *ciao*. Who knows when we might see each other next. Although I expect you to stay in touch.'

Xavier led her inside to the living room, where Tia had pointlessly flung open the French doors to let in the warm, fragrant air of a perfect sunny day.

'I always loved this house,' Xiomara said,

glancing around appreciatively. She stepped around in a graceful arc, her fingers gliding over cushions, a marble topped table, the framed photo of Xavier with his army unit. 'Although I only stayed here a handful of summers. But I love what you've done with it even more. It seems so much lighter than I remember.'

'The décor was a little dark for my taste,' he said woodenly. 'Plus, back then, I planned to sell the place, so I was redecorating to appeal to potential buyers.'

And now that Lola had moved out, he knew he wouldn't be able to stay for much longer. He saw her in every room, on every piece of furniture. Her playful smile, her challenging quips, her delighted laughter and her looks of what he now realised was love.

Xavier swallowed, sickened, choked by the realisation of what he'd had for one terrifying, euphoric second when she'd said those words and what he'd thrown away by being too scared to be as open as she needed him to be. Too scared to offer himself to her, flaws and all, and hope that he was enough.

'I know how you must have struggled with the lies and the betrayal and the hurt of the past,' Xiomara said in her forthright way.

She was much like Lola, this half-sister of his.

'But I think you might be the second best thing

our father ever did,' she finished, turning to him, her eyes bright.

Xavier frowned, unable to address her compliment or the way she'd said *our father*, as if she truly considered him a sibling.

'What was the best thing?' he asked on a croak around the lump in his throat.

She pressed her hand to her chest and batted her eyes. 'Me, of course.' Then she fell serious once more. 'I can see that something bad has happened to you since we were last together.'

Xavier ducked his head, lacking the words to even begin to explain what he'd done or hadn't done, which was worse. He should have fought harder to keep Lola. He should have somehow found the right words to tell her how he felt. He should have begged her to stay.

'If you want advice from a wise little sister…' she said, '…here it is. Whatever you've done, fix it.'

His stare met hers, his body frozen with grief and indecision. Could he fix it? Was he capable? Could he say something to win Lola back?

'Don't throw it all away because that might seem like the least painful option,' the princess went on. 'It won't be.'

She might have meant the estate, the title, the wealth, but Xavier had a sneaking suspicion she meant Lola. It seemed female intuition was universal among the women of his life.

'Love is everything,' she said quietly, the truth of her words shining in her eyes. 'You'll soon learn that when your son or daughter arrives, as our cousin Tavi has learned it.'

Xavier stayed silent. Lola's accusations that he wanted her only for their child, slaying him anew. Even if there was no baby, he would feel this way, as if he'd never be the same again, because she was gone.

'What use is anything else in life, if you don't have someone to share it with?' Xiomara said, once more glancing around the beautiful home that meant nothing to him, not without Lola.

Xavier swallowed, aware that a response might be polite. 'Spoken like a true newly-wed,' he said, trying to smile while his heart cracked into pieces.

'Of course, it's not just anyone,' the princess continued, 'it's that special person who feels like home, no matter where the wind takes you.'

Xavier sucked in a breath, the princess's words striking at the heart of him. Lola was home. Without her this place was just like any other place, just stone and mortar. A shell. Or a cage. And Xavier didn't want to be trapped alone, missing her, aching for her, safe but bereft.

Because *she* was his place of belonging. *She* was the home he'd been searching for his whole adult life. She was *everything*. And he'd let her walk away because he'd been scared and desperate to protect himself.

'Lola is an impressive woman,' Xiomara said softly, as if aware of the chaos inside him, as if he were indeed made of glass. 'I hope you find a way to make your little family work.'

Xavier snapped out of his trance. Xiomara was leaving. She would take her female intuition and wisdom with her and he still needed to know how to fix it with Lola.

'How…? What…?' He swallowed and tried to get the question out. 'What does it feel like? How do you know it's enough?'

Xiomara raised her eyebrows, a small smile playing on her lips. 'Love?'

Xavier nodded.

'It feels like you look,' she said sympathetically. 'As if you're at the centre of a terrible storm, but you've never been more ecstatically alive.'

Xavier exhaled the breath he'd been holding, his body sagging with exhaustion. So this, the way he'd been feeling for weeks but denying, was love?

'I know…' Xiomara said. 'It's wonderful, isn't it?'

Wonderful? Xavier shook his head, feeling as if he might pass out. He'd already loved Lola but he'd let her go, too scared to say the words.

'Does she love you, too?' she whispered, perhaps sensing how close he was to utterly breaking down.

He nodded. 'She did. But…' He'd failed her, his

love too little, too late. She'd finally seen through him and found him lacking as he'd feared.

'It's not too late to tell her how you feel,' Xiomara said.

He looked up sharply. 'Isn't it? How can you be sure?'

'She's having your baby, Xavier. She's been living here with you. She's put her career on hold to make this, the three of you as a family, work.'

He nodded, restless energy boiling inside him. He needed to go to Lola now. To tell her he loved her back and beg her to give him another chance, because without her, he couldn't breathe.

'I have to go,' Xiomara said. 'Remember, if you ever need anything, I expect you to reach out to your only sister, first and foremost.'

Xavier took her hands in his when she offered them.

'I'll see you soon,' she said, once more pressing her cheeks to his. 'Don't see me out. I don't do goodbyes, so *cuídate*,' she said, sweeping towards the hall as she waved over her shoulder.

And just like that, Xavier was once more alone with the knowledge that, through his own fear and inaction, he might have lost the best thing that had ever happened to him and his only chance to be happy.

CHAPTER SEVENTEEN

From her sun-filled kitchen, Lola abandoned her untouched and now cold tea and sighed. The movers were arriving later today to put all her worldly possessions into storage. Now that she'd left Xavier and Casa Colina, left behind a relationship that was going nowhere, her life was supposed to be getting back on track. Her feelings for him dying. Except her restlessness, the certainty that she would love him for ever, grew stronger, hour by hour.

Needing to hear a friendly voice, she called Isla. The call connected and the hollowness inside her expanded as she wished more than anything, that her sister was there, in the flesh.

'Are you okay?' Isla asked, as instinctively in tune with her twin as ever, as if they shared an emotional barometer.

'I'm in love,' Lola said with a wince, her throat aching with unshed tears. 'And it's over.'

'Oh, *manita*… I'm sorry,' Isla said. 'Tell me what happened.'

Lola recounted the events of the day of the wedding, the moment she'd realised she'd fallen deeply in love with the father of her baby and he didn't love her back.

'I had to leave,' she said, recalling the look of hurt and devastation on Xavier's face when she'd told him her feelings. 'I couldn't do it any longer. Pretend. I can't love him, live with him and have no more than the thing I threw away when I was nineteen. A loveless relationship where he wants me only for the baby. Only so his massive house doesn't feel so empty. For appearances. He doesn't want *me*.'

'Did he say he doesn't love you?' Isla asked cautiously.

'No. He didn't have to.' Doubts chipped away at her memories of how he'd looked that night. 'He can't love anyone, or won't. He won't let me in.' Lola dropped her head into her hand, the look on his face when she'd told him he wasn't enough for her haunting her still. 'I can't believe I'm back here, in love with someone who doesn't love me in return. In love with someone who only wants me for the way I make his life better.' Except the situations were different. She'd hadn't loved Nicolás the way she loved Xavier.

'Is he scared?' Isla asked.

'Probably. And I get it, you know. I'm scared too. I thought I was in love with Nicolás, but that was just childish infatuation. Nothing close to the way I feel about Xavier. I mean I'm having his baby. We worked together. We were sleeping together and living together. What did he expect me do, if not fall for him?'

'What are *you* scared of?' Isla whispered, the beats of silence after her question making Lola's pulse throb in her temples.

'I guess I was scared of making another mistake. Of loving him so hard, that I would lose myself. That I'd become nothing more than part of a couple when I've always had bigger dreams.'

'Would that be so bad?' Isla challenged. 'To be a part of a couple with the man you love? To be part of a family with the man you love? You've always wanted what Mamá and Papá have. Ask yourself, which regret would be the biggest?' Isla pushed. 'That you never had your career or that you never knew the kind of love you're in right now?'

Lola gasped softly, certain of the answer, feeling stupid that with a bit of distance and some wisdom from the only other person who knew her so well, everything suddenly made sense. She didn't have to choose because she could have both. She didn't have to be scared she'd become something intolerable because she made good decisions. She didn't have to run away from her fears. She could embrace them and risk everything, knowing the reward was worth it.

'It's not even as if he forced me to choose,' she

told Isla. 'He'd never do that, never expect me to be something I'm not. He wants me to be safe and happy...'

'Sounds to me like he is in love with you. Maybe he just hasn't realised it, or maybe he just struggles to talk about his feelings.'

'He does.' Lola nodded, her eyes stinging with tears. 'He's scared that he can't love because his father rejected him and he doesn't belong. But he *does* belong. With *me*.'

'Did you tell him that?' Isla asked.

Lola stood and paced, too restless to sit. 'No... not exactly. I told him I loved him then I said his best wasn't enough for me and ran away.'

An uncomfortable moment of silence passed where hot shame washed over Lola. She'd hurt him too, rejected him out of her own fear. Instead of sitting down with him and calmly confessing her feelings, giving him a chance to assimilate them and respond.

'You asked me what he expected of you,' Isla said, 'but I think you already know the answer to that question.'

'He expected me to reject him,' Lola whispered, scrunching her eyes closed as if she could obliterate the image of Xavier's pain. 'Oh no...' What had she done...? 'I'm sorry. Can I call you later? I have to go.' She jerked to her feet.

'Then stop talking to me and go and get the life you want, the way you always have.'

'I love you,' Lola said. 'Thanks for listening.'
'You're welcome.'
Then Lola ran.

The only place Xavier could think to look for Lola when there was no response at her apartment, was the *Clinico San Carlos*. He reasoned she might have loose ends to tie up. Only no one there had seen her, nor were they expecting her given that she was no longer an employee.

As he drove back towards Casa Colina, his gut churning with impotence, frantic that she might have already gone to Spain while he'd been wallowing, he broke the promise he'd made to her and dialled her number. She'd begged him for space. But he couldn't let her go another second thinking that he was done fighting for her, for them.

After two rings, the call connected. He almost sobbed with relief. 'Lola, where are you? I need to speak to you. I know I said I'd give you space but...' His throat closed, all the feelings he'd repressed fighting to be set free.

'I'm on my way back,' she said. 'I've just pulled through the gates. I'll be with you in two minutes.'

'You're at Casa Colina?' he asked, his brain sluggish but hope choking him.

'Yes,' she said urgently.

'Stay there,' he said, his heart in his throat. 'Don't leave. I'm not at home but I'll be right behind you.'

He tore along the coastal road, impatiently waiting for the gates to his property to open. Then with a final skid of gravel, he sped down the drive, leaving the engine running and the car door open in his haste to get to Lola.

He found her in the kitchen with Tia, who took one look at Xavier and discreetly left the room.

'You came back,' he said, stepping forward, his arms aching to hold her and never let her go again.

She nodded, her eyes wary. 'I should never have left. I'm sorry, Xavier.'

'Why?' He frowned, confused, overwhelmed by his feelings, which were surely too big for any man to survive. 'I'm the one who needs to apologise.'

She shook her head. 'No, *I* do. I told you that you weren't enough when you are. You're everything I want.'

'Lola—'

'No. I should have given you time. I should have told you that it's okay to not have the answers. That I'm scared too.'

'I'm only scared of losing you.' He gripped her shoulders, his hands restlessly caressing them to make sure she was real. 'I don't just want you for the baby. I don't just want you to help me run this estate. I'd live anywhere as long as it's with you.'

Lola placed her hands on top of his, her stare awash with tears. 'Xavier...'

'Please let me speak.' He cupped her face. 'I'm

sorry it took me so long to recognise what was going on inside me. I'm sorry that I kept you out and hurt you, because I was so scared that you would see something in me that was unlovable. I was scared that I'd try to love you and it wouldn't be enough. But I know now, what this feeling is.' He pressed his fist to his breastbone. 'I already love you, Lola. I have for weeks. I love you. *You* are where I belong. *You* are my family. You and the baby. I never want to be anywhere else but at your side. Wherever that is.'

Tears spilled over her lashes and he dragged her into his arms. His heart recognising the rhythm of hers, breathing in the scent of her, coming home.

'You don't have to say it back,' she said, looking up at him. 'It's okay to be confused.'

'I'm no longer confused. And it's true. I love you. It's like you said. When you know it's right, you want to fight for it. Give it everything you have. I know this is right. *You* are right. You are the person I'll love for the rest of my life and I don't want to be without you for another second.'

Then he kissed her.

From the courtyard, Lola snuggled closer into Xavier's side as they watched the sun set over the bay. The sky streaked with pink and orange. Her heart finally whole.

'Will you stay?' he asked, one hand holding

hers, their fingers entwined, the other stroking her back.

'Of course,' she said, never wanting to be anywhere else but in his arms.

'Not at Casa Colina, but with me,' he looked down at her, his dark eyes gleaming with the feelings she'd waited so long to see. 'For ever?'

'Yes,' she replied, pressing her lips to his. 'I love you. I'll never leave you ever again.'

He cupped her face, his stare intense. 'You know I'd love you even if there was no baby, don't you? You know that I love the woman you are, just as you are and never want you to be anything but yourself?'

She nodded, desperate not to cry again.

'I'm sorry that I protected myself so well,' he went on. 'That I almost ruined the best thing that's ever happened to me. You. The thing I've been searching for my entire life. Belonging.'

'And I'm sorry...' she whispered, '...that I compared what we have with the things of my past. This, us, my love for you. It's everything I want. It's the thing that's been missing from my life. The thing I've felt restless for. *You* are what's been missing and you will always be enough.'

He took her hand, pressed a kiss to the centre of her palm and then pressed her hand over his heart. 'I'm yours. And now that I've found you, now that I've woken up and realised I'm not broken or unlovable, I'm never letting you go.'

She leaned close and kissed him, her love swelling inside her so he was all she saw, all she needed. Their kissing turned heated, the urgency of every touch and caress building until there was only one way to contain the fire—with their passion.

'Hold on,' Xavier said as he gripped her thighs and stood, carrying her.

She wrapped her arms and legs around him as he headed upstairs, laying her down against the cool linens of his bed where he slowly stripped her, caressing every inch of her body with his hands and kisses and flicks of his tongue and they loved each other all night long to seal the promises they'd made.

EPILOGUE

Two years later

HAND IN HAND with Xavier, as the sun set on a stunning late summer's day, Lola trailed behind their dark-haired toddler as they walked between the Casa Colina vines, inspecting the grapes for the upcoming harvest.

'I think it will be a good year,' Xavier said, plucking a fat black grape from the vine and pressing it to Lola's lips for her to taste, his stare, as always, full of love and passion.

In the two years since they'd made Casa Colina their permanent home, Xavier had attended university to learn all about viticulture and loved showing off his new talents.

She parted her lips, smiling as the sweetness of the fruit burst on her tongue. Then, with one eye on Gabriel, who'd they'd named after the storm that had brought them together, she wrapped her arms around Xavier's shoulders and pressed her body as close to him as possible given the constraints of her heavily pregnant belly.

'Every year with you is a good one. A gift.' She brushed her lips over his, smiling when his hands spread over her ribs, clutching her to him as he groaned softly into their kiss.

The baby nestled between them chose that moment to stretch and kick and they laughed together, breaking apart but holding hands.

Xavier dropped his other hand to her belly and rested it over their daughter, who was due any day now. 'She agrees with me about the vintage,' he said with a smile.

'Maybe wine making will be in her blood.' She smiled at him indulgently because they'd made a good life for themselves, supporting each other's dreams and ambitions. Lola had gone back to work part time after Gabriel was born and she planned to squeeze in that master's degree when her current maternity leave came to an end.

'What about Mira?' he asked, expectantly, suggesting another name for the baby because they'd yet to decide on one. 'Mamá said that was what she'd planned to call me, if I'd been a girl.'

'Oh... I like that.' She held his hand and they continued their evening walk, strolling behind Gabriel who toddled ahead, finding joy in every blade of grass, every fluttering insect and simply the sheer act of running.

'Depending on where you're from…' Xavier said, '…it means wonder, or ocean, or a female ruler.' He scooped up a giggling Gabriel into his arms and kissed their son's chubby angelic cheek, holding him out to Lola so she could do the same.

'Now I definitely like it,' she said, loving him harder because, as she'd predicted, he was a wonderful father. His capacity for love and patience seemingly endless.

'One to think about then,' he said. 'Right, young man, time for bed. You have a play date with your cousins tomorrow.'

Gabriel was regularly invited to play with his royal cousins, Princes Rafael and Rodrigo, at the palace. Like Lola, Queen Phoebe was expecting again and Princess Xiomara was also pregnant with her first child. Their family, the next generation of de la Rosas, was growing and Xavier finally seemed comfortable with his place in it. Although whether they attended the grandest palace ball or a private afternoon tea with the princess, he always had one eye on the security.

Of course, Lola loved that about him, as much as she loved every other part of him and always would.

* * * * *

If you missed the previous story in the Royally Tempted trilogy, then check out

Forbidden Fling with the Princess
by Amy Andrews

And if you enjoyed this story, check out these other great reads from JC Harroway

The Midwife's Secret Fling
Secretly Dating the Baby Doc
Nurse's Secret Royal Fling
Her Secret Valentine's Baby

All available now!